The Prickling

By

M.A. Savino

&

Cover Art

by

Frina Art

Table of Contents

Chapter One-Useful Senses 7
Chapter Two-Ruger's Return 15
Chapter Three-His Touch 27
Chapter Four-Broken 35
Chapter Five-Song of Sadness 45
Chapter Six-Seek 51
Chapter Seven-Free 61
Chapter Eight-Flowers 69
Chapter Nine-The Interview 77
Chapter Ten-Scolded 85
Chapter Eleven-The Storm 91
Chapter Twelve-A Secret Worth Keeping 99
Chapter Thirteen-Going Home 107
Chapter Fourteen-Run 117
Chapter Fifteen-Bait and Switch 125
Chapter Sixteen-Scene of the Crime 133
Chapter Seventeen-Safe 143
Chapter Eighteen-Not Ashley 151
Chapter Nineteen-Lonely 159
Chapter Twenty-Let Him In 167
Chapter Twenty-One-The Story 175
Chapter Twenty-Two-Sting 185
Chapter Twenty-Three-Unraveling 195
Chapter Twenty-Four-Expecting 203
Chapter Twenty-Five-The Dark Room 213
Chapter Twenty-Six-Fractured 221

Chapter Twenty-Seven-New Plan 229
Chapter Twenty-Eight-Pattern 237
Chapter Twenty-Nine Separation 245
Chapter Thirty-Power 253
Chapter Thirty-One-The Darkroom 263
Chapter Thirty-Two-Breaking Point 271
Chapter Thirty-Three–Play Ball 277
Chapter Thirty-Four-Arson 287

Chapter One–Useful Senses

Tears soaked my blinder as I cried through my muzzle. A small amount of light filtered through the cloth, and a splashing waterfall on my left made me turn my head.

The falling water's sound soon disappeared and became replaced by the crunching of stones and gravel under my kidnapper's feet.

The rain began as a mist but gave way to a soaking downpour that flooded my back like a weighted cold blanket.

The odor of wet, fallen leaves dampened my nostrils with their fragrance as the man's pace quickened across the earth's slippery top.

He walked for hours before dropping me on the rock-laden ground like a pile of trash and giving me water.

I parted my lips to speak, but he pulled the tie back over my face, and I lost my chance. Wood thudded piece by noisy piece near my head, making me cringe. I jumped whenever a new one joined the last.

My body prickled with goosebumps as the air turned cold, and darkness took the place of the visible light through my blindfold. The unique strike of a match lighting soon revealed the garbled silhouette of fire growing nearby. The man seized me by the legs and pulled me closer to its warmth without letting go. He sat in silence with his hand resting on my thigh as I shivered. Then rubbed it, providing heat with his friction.

When I stopped shaking, the man removed his hand, and utensils clanked against a pot by the fire. In a matter of minutes, the aroma of food permeated the air, making my stomach growl like an animal protecting its territory.

Each time he took a bite, the sound of his teeth sliding across a metal utensil made me cringe.

My gag came down without warning, and something came to my lips. I stuck my tongue out to assess the food for edibility, and the man thrust something salty into my mouth. I bit down on a chunk of potato that reminded me of the salt potatoes they used to serve at the county fair. Its slight, buttery consistency is a welcoming addition to my empty stomach.

I opened my mouth again, but this time something with the consistency of pork with a dash of seasoning filled my palate.

Wrappers crumpled into a bag, and I knew the restraining fabric would be returning. I did something that one wouldn't think to do; I used my manners and thanked him. The mouth cover paused before my lips as my kidnapper hesitated, then put it in place.

I'm not sure what I expected. Most people would have said, 'you're welcome.'

Instead of responding, he came so close to my face that the air from his breath moved the hair on my cheek. Chills spread throughout my body like a wave.

He dragged his fingers across my textured and bumpy arm with calculated precision. I recoiled like a reflex, and my face stung with a sudden slap. He cupped his hand back on my arm as he used it to travel from my shoulder to my hand, ceasing on my fingertips.

The drastic awareness of his eyes on me made it difficult to relax. My jaw fluttered up and down, wanting to chatter my teeth, but it couldn't because of the cloth stopping it. As I listened to the crackling sound of the fire beside us, I wondered how long he would let me live.

There were three red flags, and I ignored them all. The flat tire, the black widow that crawled across my hand, the fall that nearly killed me. The three signs, like the strikes in baseball, took me out of the game of life and straight into the hands of this stranger. I should've listened to that voice inside me.

The one saying, 'Turn around, Ashley, this is not a good idea.' But I didn't listen and climbed the mountain with my Doberman Ruger, anyway. This trip's importance outweighed the pit that grew in my stomach.

I had to decide whether to stay with my boyfriend, Ethan, or not. Why would I waste my time with someone who doesn't care about my feelings?

My tears were not only for myself. They were for Ruger. I prayed he would safely find Ethan and remembered his hide-and-seek training so they could find me before it was too late.

Exhaustion took over my body like a virus you didn't intend to catch, and sleep came without help. Oxygen-deprived air choked my burning lungs awake as the man stomped out the fire that kept us warm.

I tried to move, but the ground tortured my body with pain, holding me still.

The man took me under my arms, tossed me over his shoulder, and climbed. I imagine carrying a person straight up takes incredible strength, something this man possesses. I waited for him to drop me, deciding I was too heavy, and he couldn't climb any longer. Drop me after deciding I was not worth the struggle, but it didn't happen.

Plummeting water spilled over us, and his steps echoed as we entered a cool, floral-scented damp space.

After a few minutes of walking, he slid me off onto the ground, took me by the ankles, and dragged my body across sandy soil. I screamed through my blocked opening when his hand squeezed my swollen and bruised ankle.

When he stopped, he pulled me upright, untied my hands, and attached them so far above my head that my feet barely stirred the ground. The unmistakable sound of scissor blades opening and closing sent a wave of panic through me.

Prepared to accept my inevitable death, I relaxed my body and allowed it to hang like freezer meat from my restraints.

He didn't butcher me as expected. The man cut off my shirt and pants, then took off my hiking boots and socks. My trembling frame couldn't fold in on itself because of the bindings.

The cool air chilled me, raising the hair across every bare surface that I carry. His unbearable closeness and a hint of mint emanating from his breath made me hold mine as he ran his fingers over my bumpy abdomen.

As he made his way down, his dry, scratchy hands grazed the front of my underwear, making my breath quicken. He continued until he reached my ankles, stopped, and let go. His noisy footsteps grew farther away from me, then vanished.

My wrists burned as I tugged hard on my tethers, but they wouldn't budge. So, I walked my toes forward until something textured stopped me. I stretched my foot along the curved edge of twelve attached parts, running parallel to each other until they ceased at the grainy turf.

My foot startled back from the hollowed skeleton of a long-dead body. I'm going to die. Maybe not now, but with time, my meatless body will join whoever rests in the dust beneath me.

I tried to calm my violently shaking body, but my anxiety wouldn't relent. I need to think. How can I convince this man that I'm worth saving? I thought about what I remembered about him after finding myself flopping up and down on his shoulder.

His red flannel shirt smelled clean, had no wrinkles, and looked high quality. His boots sunk deep into the mud, and the distance between me and the land appeared vast, so I believed he was tall. I thought I smelled detergent or a cologne scent, but maybe not.

Airy sounds of wind and dripping water filled my ears as I eavesdropped on my surroundings. Taking in a deep and steady sniff, the scent of roses and humid musty air confused me. I didn't think roses grew in caves or caverns.

Quick steps darted at me, stomping the ground with heavy slaps as they approached. My body stiffened, arming itself to be battered or hurt by the charging bull.

He stopped short of touching me, put his head in the crook of my neck, and gingerly sniffed it. Sloshing water struck my leg as a bucket's metallic handle hit its plastic side when it plopped beside me.

Unprepared for what happened next, nausea made its way into my esophagus, and tightness gripped my chest like a corset.

Being half nude in front of someone is not something I am comfortable with.

The man unfastened my bra, springing my size C breasts free. He slid my underwear down to the sandy earth and paused at the bottom, waiting for me to lift my feet.

I did as expected, but my abdomen tightened as he sensually massaged both hips with his thumbs. He clutched my neck tight, cutting off my airway, and shook me until I relaxed.

Rejecting his physical contact is unacceptable. I have learned my lesson. Acceptance may be the key to my survival. However, being touched by an outsider may take more bravery and strength than I have.

A stranger bathing me is not pleasant. My naked body swayed from the ceiling as he washed me from head to toe with berry-scented water. When he finished, he didn't bother to dry me.

I sensed him staring at my cold, shivering body, but he didn't touch me. After several minutes of awkward silence, he picked the bucket up and walked away, leaving me with my darkening thoughts.

Chapter Two - Ruger's Return

Ethan peered up at the steep rocks that Ashley and Ruger ascended when they left on their morning hike. Bits of fragmented rock slid down the cliff face, landing on the ground close to where he stood.

He took a few steps back to get a better vantage point of where they came from, but he saw nothing.

He contemplated whether he should do the climb but preferred to photograph the scenery from the base of the mountains, looking up toward the sky instead of the view beneath him.

Ashley is a mountaineer, and Ruger is with her, so he isn't too concerned about her being gone for so long.

He turned without hesitation as footsteps on fallen leaves crunched behind him beyond the trees. A doe stood with a face full of grass hanging from its mouth. He fluttered his lips together and gazed up at the heavens.

It could have been something worse, like a bear. After snatching a rapid photo of the deer, he ate his granola bar and thought about Ashley. She's been so distant, and it's his fault. This trip may be his last chance to prove he can be the man she wants him to be.

After setting the digital camera on a small table inside their tent, the faint woof of a canine came from somewhere in the distance, making Ethan hold his breath so that he could listen. Ruger's distinct yelp became clear as it came closer.

"Ruger… come here, boy."

Within seconds, Ruger appeared, yelping insistently at him, then ran the other way.

"Ruger? Where are you going?"

Ethan gazed at the edge that Ruger hopped on and scowled—time to put Ruger's hide-and-seek training to the test.

"Where's mommy? Find mommy."

Ruger leaped between a few rocks and vanished. Ethan retrieved his hiking bag, camera, and water bottle, took a deep breath, and rested his hand on the first stone. Ruger peeked down and started barking again, scaring the crap out of him.

"I'm coming, boy, give me a minute," he snapped at him.

Although Ethan has the strength to climb, he doesn't have the agility of a dog—especially a dog like Ruger.
Ruger appeared again above him and barked, growing impatient with his slow ascend.

"Shut up, Ruger! I'm going as fast as I can," Ethan yelled, slapping the rocks, and yelling at him in frustration.

Ethan gripped the second ledge. After an hour of hiking and following Ruger through different paths of stone and brush, he stopped in front of a six-foot-tall ridge with a metal wire strewn across its face. Ruger whiffed the ground all around, appearing confused, and began licking something on the floor.

When Ethan moved him out of the way, blood covering a rock came into his field of vision. Shifting his attention to a red-stained cloth on the terrain, he lifted it from its corners, took a snapshot, and placed it in his protective case.

"Ashley!" Ethan screamed as he listened for any hint of noise, but none came.

He peered at Ruger and gave him the command once more.

"Ruger, find mommy. Where's Ashley?" He asked as Ruger turned his head to the side, sniffed the earth's surface, and took off with Ethan on his heels. "That's my boy."

The vicious landscape made keeping up with the dog's agile physique virtually impossible, but Ethan pressed on. After sprinting between boulders and trees, almost slipping off a cliff into the abyss, they reached their destination. Ruger snuffed and whined at something besides a rushing creek.

A gravitational blood drop splattered onto a flat stone near the creek's edge, and he swiped it with his pointer finger.

Ethan traced the different splatters until they disappeared into the water. He ran through the water to the other side, searching for more red droplets, but found none. He turned to the expansive green and multicolored valley in one direction and then to the vast elevations and cliffs in the other.

No signs of human life besides himself existed for miles.

"Come on, boy. Where's mommy?" He chirped.

Ruger traveled a few feet past a line of bushes, then stopped in front of pieces of cut wire on the ground with a splash of blood nearby.

Fingers gouged the turf under the gravel surface, leaving their purposeful mark and unsettling the landscape.

"Ashley…. Ashley... Ashley..." His screaming, repetitive words echoed through the trees next to the mountain and the valley below, but no response besides his own came from them.

He needed to climb down the trail and return to civilization, so he took a stick and carved her a message. Spelling out, 'went for help,' followed by the letter 'E' with a branch. He dropped stones in the grove to keep the words from washing away.

Anytime he left her a note when he went someplace, he would sign it 'E,' and she would do the same and sign it with 'A.'

Once certain his letters would remain, Ethan turned his thoughts to finding his way back for help.

Ruger ran by his side as they came back to the cliff ledge. This is where Ethan paused, but Ruger dove off without a second thought.

He would break his leg if he tried to make that leap.

Ethan took several deep breaths, sat down on his bottom, rolled himself onto his stomach, with his legs dangling over, and descended carefully.

He grappled the sharp rock with a firm grip, preparing to drop, when Ruger, without warning, snatched his pant leg and forced him down.

The force of his pull caused him to land hard on his ass.

"Dammit, Ruger," Ethan sneered.

The scorching sun shined on his irritated face as he reprimanded the dog. He snatched his water and took a few gulps before mustering up the energy to stand.

A sharp ache cut like a knife as an old back injury from a car accident reignited like gasoline on a fire. While bending over to retrieve his bag, a bat-to-the-back-like agony brought him to his knees.

"Shiiiiiiiit," he shrieked.

He bent his legs to pick up his backpack, this time without using his back, and continued his journey. The uneven obstacles made climbing down almost unbearable. Ethan furrowed his brow as he continued his descent.

After climbing and hiking for an hour, he arrived at their campsite. Ruger waited by his bowl for food, wiggling his nub. Ethan gave him a handful of kibbles, packed some valuables, and started down the treacherous route back to the park entrance to find help.

As he crossed the parking lot, a park ranger approached him in a pickup and rolled down his window.

"Excuse me, sir, the dog needs a leash," the ranger ordered, pointing at Ruger.

"I understand, but I need help. My girlfriend has disappeared." Ethan said frantically.

"She's missing?"

"Yes. Ashley went on a hike with our dog. The dog came back, but she didn't."

"Well, the dog could have run off without her. Is the site on the mountain?" The ranger asked.

"Yes, but I think she's hurt. I found blood," Ethan said, pulling out the red-stained towel and passing it to him. "Here, see."

The ranger took the fabric Ethan handed him in its corner, rotated it, and shook his head. The man's weathered tan face looked like that of an old messenger pouch out in the elements far too long, and his unpressed, wrinkled pants longed to be washed. Dandruff floated down the ranger's forest-colored shirt like lake-effect snow as he shook his head and eyed Ethan suspiciously.

"Listen, darkness is dangerous, and they won't send anyone out this late in this terrain."
"So, what, you're doing nothing?" Ethan asks, throwing his hands up in the air in frustration. "This is bullshit."
"Now listen. Nobody said nothing would be done. Put the pup in the back, and hop in. We can go as close to the campsite as possible. Then walk the rest of the way and take a gander. Who knows, she may even be there when we arrive. Things like this happen often," the ranger told him, pushing the passenger side door of his truck open.
"And if she isn't?" Ethan says, hesitating before getting in.
The ranger sucked his rat-like teeth and replied, "I can call in the report, and the search party can find her when the sun comes up."

Ethan secured Ruger in the truck's cargo bed and climbed beside the ranger.

"Mint?" The ranger offered, handing him a green sleeve of spearmint breath mints.

"No thanks," Ethan uttered, waving off the sweaty opened tube. "I have gum."

The bumpy drive back up the mountain almost killed him. Ethan's unstable back went from some discomfort to stabbing with every harsh pothole. Ethan grimaced and sucked air through his teeth with each bounce of the truck's cab. When the road stopped being drivable, the ranger pulled over, and Ethan hopped out and stretched to take the strain out of his uncooperative spine. The ranger went around Ethan's side and scrunched his thick brow.

"What's the problem, sir? Sorry, I didn't get your name. I'm Oliver." The ranger extended his hand to him.

"Ethan, and it's my back. It's on fire," he said, shaking his hand.

"I have something that'll help, but if anyone asks, it didn't come from me. Understand?"

"Trust me; I'm not telling. I might need more if I plan to make it through the weekend," Ethan said.

"Ashley, is your girlfriend's name, right?" Oliver asked as he opened the door to his truck and removed a prescription from the glove compartment.

"Yes," Ethan answered, reaching his hand to accept the round white circular tab marked with a ten. "What is this?"

"A pain pill leftover from surgery last year. I only take them if I'm in dire straits, which you appear to be in now. Swallow that, and all discomfort vanishes," Oliver chuckled.

Ethan glanced at the tablet apprehensively, unscrewed his water bottle, and chugged it down. He needed the throbbing to go away.

"So, which way?" Oliver asked, pointing at the general area around them.
"Over this way."

Ruger ran ahead of them. Ethan and Oliver walked most of the way without exchanging words until the ranger broke the quiet.

"How long have you and Ashley been together?" He inquired.
"About a year, I guess."
"A year? That's not bad. Camp together often?" Oliver asked Ethan, who halted abruptly.
"Am I a suspect?" Ethan replied with his hands on his hips.
"Hey, we are just two men talking here. I'm not implying anything. I am just passing the time," the ranger said with his hands up in defeat.

They trudged the rest of the way in silence until they reached their tent. Ruger sat waiting beside his food bowl, so Ethan scooped a cupful and filled his dish. The ranger meandered around inside the tent and picked up Ethan's camera.

"Can I see what's on here?"

"I'm not sure how it helps, but yes," Ethan said, opening the media file. "Just be careful. This is a costly piece of equipment."

"If it's so expensive, why leave it here?" Oliver asked without looking.

"Because if Ashley did come back, she would know I'm coming back too."

"Is this her?" Oliver inquired, turning the camera to him. "The redhead?"

"Yes."

"She's a beautiful girl. You're a lucky guy. Is she a model or something?" Oliver quizzes, giving him back his prized possession.

"Thanks, and no, Ashley is not. She should have been, though," Ethan said, taking it from him. "She's a paralegal."

"Are there any signs of her presence?" Oliver said, irritated.

"No. It appears the same," Ethan said, looking around.

"Missing persons dispatch it is," Oliver said, grabbing his phone. "I need some basic information before calling."

"Whatever is required," Ethan offered.

After providing the ranger with Ashley's demographics for the report, Ethan sat on a downed

24

tree nearby, petting Ruger, while the ranger made the call. The stars started twinkling above him while he waited.

He gripped his camera, attached a wide-angle adapter, and took several night skies images.

Ashley would have loved the view if she were here. What is he going to say to her? She tried hard to get him to go on the hike, but he declined.

Now, he's alone on their weekend camping adventure, and she's missing because of him.

The ranger strolled over, stopped before him, and stared at the moon.

"Beautiful, isn't it?" he said, placing his phone in his breast pocket.

"Magnificent," Ethan said, putting his adapter back in its box.

"The information has been communicated, and at first light, they are coming up to start the search. I suggest staying here in case she comes back. I'm heading out if it's all right."

"Fine with me," Ethan said with pin-point eyes.

"Medicine kicked in, didn't it?" The ranger smirked.

"Sure did," Ethan revealed, smiling.

"Well, don't get used to it. I can't give out any more, so if any wood chopping needs to be done, do it now while you're numb," Oliver shouted over his shoulder before disappearing through the trees leading to his vehicle.

Ethan picked up a flashlight and headed into the woods to gather logs for a fire with Ruger in tow. Using his heavy-duty log carrier, he gathered enough timber to build a few fires and returned to his quarters.

After creating a bonfire, he attached Ruger to his trolley, gave him water, and took his camera for evening shots of the mountainside.

Chapter Three-His Touch

The cold chiseled into my body like an ice pick shaping a frozen sculpture. Liquid dripped nearby, and echoes of falling water filled the cave-like space with surround sound, much like a theater.

I pulled at my arm bindings, but the painful brush burns from earlier attempts stopped me. The rhythmic throbbing of my ankle matched my beating heart beneath me as I cried. A break in the sound of the falling water made me tense with sudden surprise.

He's coming...

His heavy steps quickened and grew louder and faster as he approached me. My breaths hyperventilated through my nostrils as I braced myself for death's unseen weapon again, but nothing happened.

He circled me like a shark circling its prey before it bites and tears its meal to pieces. The aromatic scent of rose came from his direction.

Every time he passed in front of me as he circled, I caught a whiff of floral. The sudden soft touch of a flower touched me between my bare breasts.

Air stuttered out of me like cooling hot soup as he slid the velvety petal down my abdomen, skirted it around my labia, and swiping it softly.

I didn't want to react, but my neglected body had a mind of its own.

This seemed to please him as he clucked his tongue on the roof of his mouth and continued to caress my skin with the rose. He made his way around to the back side of my body and traced it from top to bottom down my crevice.

I shuttered in response and could feel myself wanting more.

What is wrong with me? Has it been so long that my denied body is enjoying a stranger's touch?

His lips tenderly kissed my left buttock, and I flinched my body forward, unintentionally forgetting the rules.

He grabbed my hips hard, digging his fingertips into them and pulling me back. His mouth took hold of a cheek and sucked it as his arms came around my waist and pulled me into him.

I relaxed my body in acceptance of his control, and he rewarded me by letting go.

His steps came in front of me, and hot breath warmed my textured body as he made his way to the in-between and stopped. My body shook with anticipation as his mouth hovered before my sopping pleasure zone.

I wanted him when I shouldn't. I needed him to touch me, even though it felt wrong, but my mind and body worked independently, and I'm out of control.

I battled it from the inside and tried to think of something so undesirable that my feelings of sensuality would dissipate, but I failed.

My neglected body has been without true intimacy and intense desire for so long that it didn't work.

Exploding into his mouth violently as he shoved his tongue inside me, I burst into tears for inappropriately reacting to his sexual assault.

A quiet moan came from him, and I tried to decipher its meaning as he consumed me.

Is this for his pleasure or mine? Either way, I couldn't breathe. The air inside my lungs became stuck.

Abandoning all feelings of right and wrong, my mind wandered away, releasing itself as he pleasured me. No one had ever touched me like this, so my body overacted to every new thing he did to me.

I'm ruined for anyone else now. If they tried to do any of this to me, I would fold like a bad hand at a poker game, pushing them away.

I thought there would be more to come when he removed his head, but he vanished as I dangled with inappropriate satisfaction from the cave ceiling. I wished Ethan had touched me like that. But that's not who he is. Sure, we have sex, but it's just that, sex. We have no connection in the way that we should.

Everything else about my and Ethan's relationship is perfect, except for his lack of intimacy. Our sex life, although superficial, satisfied his needs without mentally relinquishing his emotional side and heart to me.

I wanted that from him more than anything in the world. I needed him to trust me enough to give in to his desires and let me have all of him instead of the bits and pieces he gives me now.

My abdomen twisted in knots, and bile made its way into my esophagus as I became aware of how much I enjoyed the stranger's touch.

Although the act destroyed me, I wanted more in a disgusting, inappropriate way. I'm glad he left. It gave me time to scream and thrash about without fear of the consequences of my actions.

I didn't mind being alone, but being alone naked in this cold cave made me feel like bait for another animal. I waited to be attacked, waited to be devoured, waited for death.

A chilly breeze drifted past me, and so did the scent of food. I am trying to remember when he fed me last, but it seemed a long time since I ate. Perhaps this is part of his torture. He sits outside the cave beyond the falls next to a warm fire and feasts on a lavish meal as I wither away and starve. Marching feet advanced in my safe space, ceasing before me.

My gag came down, and he pressed a cup to my lips. Sweet strawberry wine washed my palette, sweetening my taste buds as I swallowed. He continued serving me until the cup ran dry, then replaced the fabric cover over my mouth.

I wanted food but didn't receive it. Instead, my head became heavy, and my legs weakened. My bound hands tightened, and my body hung loosely, unable to support itself.

The man hoisted my compliant frame up and detached me from the ceiling. I floated down to the floor, and he dragged me by the arms a short distance until we reached a wall. He reattached my wrists to another device, bound my ankles, and pulled me straight.

I tried to draw my knees to my abdomen to get warm on the cold sandy ground, but he grabbed them, yanked them straight a second time, and rolled me onto my side.

This is where I stayed, motionless and afraid to move, as he eased himself behind my bare back and spooned me. I would never have slept if my drink had no drugs.

He squeezed me tighter when I awakened and stirred my frame beneath his arm. His warmth felt unnerving, and I adjusted awkwardly when I realized his bare body now touched me. I did not intend to disobey the rules, but I couldn't help it. He seized me by the hair and pulled me back to him.

His hand roamed to my front and traveled between my legs, where his fingers made entry and worked in and out of me. His manhood stiffened to stone behind me, and I knew he planned to take me.

I flailed my body like a fish out of water, trying to stop it, but my vain efforts did little as he pushed me onto my stomach and forced himself into me from behind.

His sizeable shaft slammed into me repeatedly while he ignored my outward cries. Sand stung my face with every forward thrust of his body into mine, harder and harder, as if he hated me.

The painful encounter lasted for several minutes until he finally collapsed heavily on top of me, panting like a dog. He moved between my thighs and took a deep whiff of our joint liquid scent emanating from my once-sacred space. I shivered at his words when he finally spoke in a low, barely discernable whisper.

"I think I'll keep you...." he said as he climbed off me.

His words cut me like a knife as I realized he might never let me go. I could hear him putting on clothes and tying his shoes. Then the silence returned as he abandoned me once more. I wept fully and without fear as I pulled and thrashed about, trying to escape.

It didn't work. Whatever I'm fastened to held like a wench pulling a car from a ditch. My weeping turned to muffled screams hoping someone would hike close enough to hear me. Even though I doubted it would get through the sound of the waterfall, I kept going until my throat became raw.

Racing feet stomped rapidly across the ground before a slap crossed my buttocks, startling me. He flipped me from a prone to supine position and grabbed me by the throat.

"Shhh... Don't make me regret my decision," he said in a hushed tone.

He let go of my neck and stroked my cheek with his finger before leaving again. My screaming must have been audible enough to summon him back to my side, so I know now that it carries enough to reach beyond the falls.

I need to wait a little longer next time before trying again. The stable sand is far better than hanging from the ceiling, but no more comforting to my mind.

I want to go home. I miss Ruger and my boyfriend, even though I planned on leaving him after this weekend if things didn't change.

I would give anything to be with him right now and gladly accept his lack of passion over a forced relationship any day, but it may never happen.

This crazed mountain man intends to keep me like a secret he never plans to share with anyone... ever.

Chapter Four-Broken

Whenever I heard a clamor, I thought it might be him returning. I have slept and awakened so many times that I don't know what day it is.

Maybe this is it. This is how I die, rotting next to the corpse beside me. Perhaps this is his plan to take my soul, my life, and my body inexplicably.

The ground beneath me is soiled with urine that my bladder no longer holds, and my shriveled lips are stuck to the gritty material in my mouth.

I think death would be easier. If someone found me like this, I would never recover from the humiliation or shame of what had happened.

A torrential rainstorm poured outside and fell through the cracks in the ceiling. It drizzled in a pattern on my skin, left, right, and back again, chilling it with every splatter. Humming to myself to pass the time, I thought about my life.

Years ago, I wanted to be a singer, but stage fright took my chances away. Now, I keep my euphonious voice to myself. I grew tired of people trying to get me to try out at singing contests and audition for dramas and plays. They never ended well, so I abandoned my calling.

Falling asleep is easy now. My dehydrated and malnourished body withered away in the dark, unable to do anything else.

When the dripping ceased, and the thunder stopped, I tried to scream one last time, but nothing came from me. I lost the power to make a sound or move, so I wept dry tears.

An abrupt loud metallic racket hitting the side of a bucket startled me to attention. The man detached my hands from the wall and pulled me by the calves through my own waste.

He lifted me by the arms, hooked me back to the roof, unbound my feet, and began scrubbing me from head to toe.

I did not move or flinch. There is nothing left of me but this empty shell of a human. The fight in me is gone, and I have accepted my fate.

After washing me, he changed my eyewear from behind. I would have looked around if I had the brawn, but I stared ahead at the layered wall. The cologne he wore smelled woodsy and sensual. It must be nice to shower and wash filth down a drain and into a sewer like a normal person.

At least he is clean and not some vagrant that never bathes, and I'm thankful for that.

His hands caressed my bottom with lotion seductively. As he applied it to my breasts and abdomen, more questionable moisture sputtered out of its container. His hands ventured downward and stopped at my feet, where he raised them gingerly, kneaded the cream in, and set them back down.

Something must have kept him from me, and he's making up for it by being tender.

When he pulled my gag down, something like water with a hint of orange flavor entered my mouth. Despite my despair, I needed my strength back, and I wanted to live.

Once he took the fluid away, he gave me chocolate pudding. It slid into my barren stomach with its astonishing tasty consistency and joined the juice right before I fainted.

Light barely filtered through my eye covering when I regained consciousness. He's holding me around the ribs, and we are on the floor again, but something is different.

My lips glided back and forth with ease. He took away the restraint, and my legs also moved freely. Although still blinded and my hands still bound, it gave me hope.

The clear echo of plummeting rocks made the man jump from beside me. He flipped me onto my back and cupped his hand across my mouth.

"Shhh…be quiet," he whispered.

I nodded my understanding, and he took his hand away. Crunching footsteps shifted, becoming louder and louder as someone made their way toward us.

The man left my side to address the intruder. Before too long, muffled bellows came through the cavity like an animal brawling for its life as I prayed for rescue.

"Help me!" I yelled with all my might but received no feedback.

Soon I realized why no one answered as something landed with a thud next to me. The distinct scent of rusty blood permeated the air. The mountain man killed whoever found us and is rifling through their pockets.

His hand came to my naked thigh and rubbed it as I sobbed. Words previously trapped inside me leaked out into the open air.

"Please, let me go."

The man threw himself on me, grasped the hair on the back of my head, and pulled my ear to his lips. His breath, winded from the battle, as he ground his lower body between my nude legs and muttered.

"Never…"

There is nothing more to say. Anyone who came, he would kill. If I hollered and drew someone to our cavern, he would take their lives, so
I remained soundless.

Plastic bags rustled next to me as the cringing sound of a swooshing saw moved forward and backward. Buzzing flies flew annoyingly around us, landing on my face and arms as the stench of decay flourished by the minute. The putrid odor became too much to bear, and I heaved.

He didn't stop dismembering. Instead, he sawed faster. Nothing came out as I continued to hurl beside him, for my hollow belly, much like this cave, held only vile contents.

Once he finished dismantling the person beside me and bagging them up, pails of water splashed next to me.

The contaminated biohazard flooded under my back and splattered on my left cheek as he rinsed the blood away from the sandy soil. After several passes, he stopped, stacked his buckets together, and walked away. When he came back moments later, he took the body-part-filled sacks away.

Death's watered-down liquids seeped into the earth underneath me and dried to my face and bare flesh. The man must have used all the water to cleanse his workspace, so I may not see him again, as he needs to replenish.

Time moved at a snail's pace while I waited for his return, and I eventually fell asleep.

As I dozed, I dreamed that what was happening was one big nightmare, a punishment for wanting to leave my job.

My boss could be such a jerk and scream and yell when things don't go his way. As his paralegal, I did all the work while he made all the money. His unpredictable moods sometimes made my days at work exhausting.

I wished he could see my value as an employee who should be treated with respect, not disdain.

Every time I planned on quitting, he would sense it and buy me lunch or offer to let me go home early. It was as though he realized he had taken his frustration out on me unintentionally and then would make up for it.

He has so much passion for his job and clients. If he weren't my boss, when he asked me out for drinks after work once, I would have said yes. But Ethan and I had just met, and dating your boss is frowned upon, no matter what company you work for.

Smiling in my dream, I walk up to my boss, punch him in the face, and tell him, 'I quit,' then slam the door behind me, shattering its glass.

Instead of getting angry, Mr. Johnston grabs me firmly and kisses me passionately on the lips.

I don't know why the dream ended that way. Perhaps it was because now I regret declining that drink and shedding Ethan from my life early in our relationship.

If only dreams came true in real life. By now, Mr. Johnston has probably fired and replaced me for not showing up to work on Monday. It will be a blessing in disguise if I make it out of this alive.

Hours soared by before the mountain man returned. It is dark, and I wonder if he has night vision goggles or if the light is too dim to travel through my filter.

He's now taken me by the arms, unhooked me, and hung me up, spread eagle, gapping my legs far apart and securing them. My feet didn't touch the ground. Suspended inches above it, I imagined I looked like a giant 'X' marking his treasure location.

I gasped when the water struck me in the chest like a drunken prisoner, hardening my nipples into diamonds that could cut glass. His fingers strummed my jewels one, then the other, toying with them, toying with me.

He scrubbed my body with clean-smelling soap and fruit-scented liquid that progressively warmed— massaging it passionately into me until it coated my dermis down to my spotless toes.

As he took off his clothes next to me, I couldn't even cry. The well inside me is empty, and whatever is about to happen doesn't matter anymore. Fighting only caused pain.

My legs went out from under me without warning, and I began hyperventilating as he hoisted them back toward the top of the vault, and removed my gag.

I dangled in the air like a skydiver descending through the clouds and making its way to the earth below. He walked around me several times, contemplating what he would do next.

I jolted at the sudden euphoric feeling of his tongue inside me. He licked and rotated it in and out of my clitoris until juices released themselves into his mouth.

As I wheezed, an outcry came from my lungs, and my body shuddered violently. He began sucking on my lips like a gourmet lollipop, then dragged his mouth appendage to my taint and across my anus.

I quivered and cried out in front of him as he lowered my legs to waist level, gripped my thighs, and made a gentle entry.

"Please, stop," I asked, through panting lips.
"I take what I want, when, and how I want. Understand?" He mumbled in a calm, hushed voice.

When I didn't answer him, he retaliated with harsh, angry thrusts that almost broke me. I yelped loudly and responded quickly.

"Yes," I screamed as his pace returned to being gentle.

Being silent is my reward. This is how I'm treated when I'm good and follow orders. This is how I stay alive.

I shut my eyes and fantasized about Ethan relinquishing himself to me. It's all I have left of him, memories. He may never want me again after this. I'm damaged goods.

The man's circular rhythm made for a quick response, and he stifled a moan as he came inside me. Semen dribbled between my legs as he pulled himself out and began dressing.

Even though he did all the work, I felt exhausted and couldn't wait for him to take me down so I could rest.

But he left me there dangling like a Christmas ornament. He didn't bother to put anything over my mouth because it was raining again, so no one would hear me.

Icy water dripped onto my spine as my head became heavy, along with my heart, so I let it rest like the rest of me.

Chapter Five-Song of Sadness

Bacon's distinct scent woke me, and my mouth watered. I am trying to remember when I ate breakfast or an actual meal.

Many days have passed, and I have lost time, so how could I be sure? This may be a mirage where I'm smelling things instead of seeing them.
I learn quickly that it isn't a figment of my imagination as the man places a crunchy piece of pork on my tongue, and I savored its salt on my palette.
The man gave me a whole strip and a couple of bites of scrambled eggs and apple juice.
Perhaps he is trying to build up my strength. But why? I'm not planning on fighting back. Ending up dead in the innermost walls of this cavern or chopped up in pieces is not on my to-do list.
Today, I needed to get through to him. I need to help him realize I am a person, not a thing he can play with when he is so inclined. Some say music soothes the savage beast, so maybe the way to his heart would be with a song. Improving his mood might earn me another meal, so it is worth a try.
Plates rattled together as he cleaned them in the buckets next to me.
Now was the time, so I wet my lips, cleared my throat, and started singing. A significant amount of time has passed since I sang aloud in front of

anyone. Not seeing helps, but the words still staggered a bit as they made their way into the air. The melody I wrote myself years ago speaks of being sad and lonely and came back to me easily.

The mountain man stopped doing dishes, stood before me, and waited for the tune to be over. His hand stroked the side of my cheek with a light touch and rubbed my dry soup coolers.

"Sing."

It's working, he wants me to keep going, but my lips and mouth are still shriveled with dehydration. He desired something from me, and I needed something from him, so I showed him my cards.

"Water," I insisted.

A burning slap struck me hard across my buttock.

"Siiiiing...," he repeated in a breathy, silent voice.
"Waaaaater," I whispered back, taunting him.

The man yelled inaudible words that echoed through the tunnel as he stomped away. He can hurt, starve, or take my body, but he can't force me to perform. This is my new power over him—tit for tat. The careful sounds of creeping footsteps made their approach. I assumed I won, but he is not giving up. Grabbing me by the angry ankle, he crushed it in his grip as I screamed, then he let go.

"Sing, now," he muttered.

Pain is a state of mind, and if I am to win this battle of wits, suffering is the only way.

"No," I whispered back.

His fingers pressed down on my inner collarbone with extreme pressure. The force caused so much agony that I almost relented.
But my shrieks pierced through the cavern, so he stopped, fearing someone might be listening.
The mountain man's heavy feet stomped the earth like a child throwing a tantrum as he walked away from me. It cost me my strength and some bruises, but it doesn't matter. Winning matters, and I am winning.
He soon returned, prepared to deal with my stubborn reluctance, and jammed me in the rib with a taser. Every muscle inside me tensed with shock, and my brain shrank to the size of a
marble rolling around in my head.

"Sing," he demanded.
"Water," I stuttered, trying to recover from the fire current flowing through me.

Another much stronger jolt made my heart flutter and rattled my backbone. Not wanting him to beat me, I remained headstrong.

He's taken enough from me, and I am not giving him anything more.

"Sing," he said through his clenched jaw.
"No."

His hollering rang out through the cave, revealing his frustration. His thumping feet advanced rapidly toward me and smacked the smile off my smug kisser.
Blood drooled onto my teeth, pooled on my lips, and fell to the ground. I lifted my head and smiled a metallic-tasting smile in his direction.
He disconnected me from the ceiling and let me fall in a heap like dirty laundry that no one wanted to touch.

"Sing or die," he said, holding a knife to my neck.
"It's hard to kill what is already dead," I smirked.

He took the blade away, replaced it with his hand, and crushed my throat. I wish he would peer into my eyes and realize I didn't fear him or death. But he wouldn't reveal himself, not even as he killed me.
I lost consciousness but didn't die, and I woke up alone without the blindfold, so I glanced around the room.
The dark cave is clean except for the skeleton in the sand. A white candle that is almost out of wax provides a small amount of light. It melted down the

side of the rock and created a semi-firm-looking puddle near the skull.

A pearl bracelet dangled from its idle hand bones, indicating it belonged to a female.

I turned my head in the other direction, and the barely visible silhouettes of more skeletons accessorized the space.

Three hung from the ceiling like Halloween decorations on a porch, and another stuck out of the earth like it tried to crawl out of a grave. My chest tightened and began shaking as an anxiety attack struck me hard. I started choking as my throat closed and my bowels released without intention.

Though my stomach was empty from several days of sparse meals, whatever I ate just emulated from my intestines. One round of foul-smelling lava drained down my cheek and emptied my bowels. The stench of my excrement made me gag, and I struggled to focus on something else to remain calm.

I glanced at the metal wires and rings attached to the cave roof where he held me. The same wire had been strewn across the face of the ledge where I caught my ankle and fell. If my body had more momentum, I would have fallen off the cliff and died. But that is not what fate had in store for me.

The sophisticated contraption had an intricate pulley system that ran on rails and appeared homemade. It is designed with a specific purpose, to keep someone a prisoner for a very long time.

I thought about the others who still hung idly from the ceiling and wondered how they died. Did they break the rules? Or did following the rules not matter because the outcome would always be the same, death?

We have more than just being trapped in this hell in common. We also each wore one item of jewelry. My mother's ring rotated on my finger as I played with it and returned to my left side.

A copperhead slithered across the sand near my legs, startling me. Uninterested in my gutless body, it ventured forward and vanished. Despite the ability to see now, I closed my eyes and listened to my surroundings. The waterfall sounded far, and a dog barked in the distance, but I
was probably hearing things.

Although still a prisoner, there are signs of progress. I'm only being held to the wall by my wrists, and the rest of me is no longer restrained. Of course, that is also the current state of the bony friends I'm surrounded by. Going back to sleep is for the best. At least there, I can dream about my freedom and enjoy life again. The problem with dreaming is that it doesn't last forever, no matter how much I wish for it.

Chapter Six-Seek

After several days of searching, the rangers still didn't find Ashley. They wouldn't let Ethan help with the search despite his repeated requests to have him use Ruger.

According to them, the damp weather and challenging terrain are too treacherous for anyone other than professionals.
It didn't stop him from offering assistance at the base of operations tent daily. His frustration mounted as a helicopter whirled overhead and multiple people milled about doing nothing. Ruger woofed at Oliver when he came too close.

"Ethan, I have explained this all before. The storms, on and off for the last several days, made everything slippery. One wrong move and splat," he said, making a slapping noise with his hands.

Ethan furrowed his brows and launched his water bottle across the lot.
A tall man in a suit with sandy brown hair snatched it up. The man stood near a blacked-out SUV, and a blond-haired woman climbed out of the passenger side. Oliver and another park employee murmured explicit words to each other.

"I wonder what they are doing here?" Oliver asked the other worker as he grimaced.

The worker didn't respond. Instead, he walked away and returned to the table with the rest of the rescue team.

"Who are they?" Ethan asked, concerned.
"Feds," Oliver answered, rolling his eyes.

The duo strolled over to them from the parking lot as Ethan continued to complain about their lack of urgency in finding his girlfriend.
Ruger planted himself between Ethan and the agents and growled through clenched teeth. The older man extended his hand, and the dog pounced, almost biting him.

"Jesus, what's his problem?"
"Sometimes he's funny with strangers," Ethan said, taking his bottle from him.
"Well, I'm Agent Barnes, and the blonde woman by the table is Mills."
"Why is the F.B.I. interested in a local woman's disappearance?" Oliver asked.
"She matches the description of five others who have vanished in the Blue Ridge Mountains in the last several years. We think the same person who took them also took her. Come with me," Barnes said, nodding for them to follow.

He nodded at Mills, and she spread out the images of the absent females. All of them have red hair, are fit and beautiful, and all went missing while hiking. Ethan picked up the image of Ashley and stroked her face with his fingers. If something happens before he can make things right, he may never forgive himself.

"Let me and my dog come," Ethan begged.

"Sir, the mountains are not safe, and the person who took Ashley is dangerous," Agent Mills said.

"We trained him to seek. We have practiced for almost a year now. He needs to be close enough, but he can do it. They've made me stand by for days, and I have seen no progress. He can do this, please. We can help," Ethan said with tears in the corners of his eyes.

"Fine, but keep the dog tied up," Barnes said.

He snatched Ruger and his pack and stood by, waiting. Oliver meandered over to object to his inclusion. He previously came to blows with Ethan when he caught him walking alone along another trail heading up the mountains. Trying to navigate at night is too risky, and they would end up searching for two people instead of one. That is why rules are in place.

"Hey, I told him he couldn't go up. He broke orders once. You're making a mistake," the ranger said.

"He's our responsibility now. We can manage him," Mills replied.

Oliver stomped away. He didn't like them taking over his investigation. He is the one that called the report in and put all these men on the mountain to help with the hunt.

Ethan waited for the duo to change their clothes into more appropriate attire for climbing.

He thought about how badly their day started before they even arrived. A nail pierced the tire on their car, and he didn't know how to change it, but Ashley did and taught him as well. She is perfect, and he wished he could express himself to her in intimate ways.

She deserved more, and he planned to work on it once he got her back home. Losing her would crush him, for he was the one with the problem. His emotional detachment disorder stems from a traumatic upbringing that he doesn't talk much about with anyone, not even Ashley.

Because he is a product of the system, he has an overwhelming fear that she will leave him or send him away, making getting close to her a challenge. His alcoholic father would beat him and his mother growing up.

Not a day passed that he or his mother didn't have a bruise or some sign of his drunken presence.

One day, his father went too far and hit her too many times, killing her. Ethan heard the entire thing and watched as his mother's blood drained under the door he was leaning against. His father ultimately killed himself, and Ethan went into the system at the age of six.

Bouncing from foster home to foster home as a child and teenager, they would bully him because of his unusual focus on cameras, their function, and photography.

He kept to himself, and most kids his age didn't understand his deep passion for the craft. Few people did until he met Ashley.

When the agents finished dressing, he and Ruger led the way up the trail.

They skidded on wet surfaces and leaves on their way back to the creek, where he left carved words for Ashley.

The stream swelled beyond its banks from all the rain and washed his message away. Ethan placed his hands on his head, frustrated.

"I put a note here, and the storm took it away. We have to get over to the other side."

"Water is too high. I'm not sure we can make it from here," Mills said as she stuck a stick in the rapids.

He went to the left, and they went to the right, looking for a good place to cross. Ruger's ears perked. He got a running start and dove across the liquid obstacle without warning. His back legs didn't quite make it, but he pulled them out of the deep water and kept going.

"Ruger!" Ethan hollered as he frantically hopped over several boulders and crossed.

The agents tried to stay on his heels, but Mills fell in, and Barnes stayed behind to help. After catching up, they ran in hot pursuit of Ruger as he raced ahead, then came to a halt near a bundle of bags on the ground. As they closed in on the packages, he growled and backed Ethan away from them with his hip.

"Ruger, move," he commanded, pushing his butt away.

His pup stepped out of the way and stood next to him, continuing to growl at the bundles of trash. Blood showed through the white plastic packages as they approached, and Mills stopped Ethan. She took white gloves out of her pocket, pulled them on, and carefully opened one. Her body hopped away from them as she covered her mouth.

"Jesus."
"What? What is it?" he asked as he walked closer to the objects.
"Human remains," she replied, taking off her gloves.

Ethan lunged toward the sacks, but Barnes held him back. Ruger jumped up and bit the agent for daring to touch his master. Blood drained from Barnes' wrist as he yelled and snatched his Glock.

"Dammit! Restrain your mutt," he screamed while holding his gun.

Ethan attached Ruger to his leash and got between Barnes and his dog.

"He's just doing his job. Lower the gun."

Barnes put the pistol away, then examined the pile himself. He removed his gloves and went to Ethan.

"The parts belong to a male," Barnes explained.

Ethan combed his fingers through his hair and let out a sigh of relief. He stood by and waited for Mills and Barnes to talk amongst themselves. The surrounding untouched area where they have ventured is unknown by many people and, therefore, natural. Pictures of this space would have fetched a high price.

He tapped his foot on the ground with crossed arms, annoyed by their secrecy. Barnes approached him, squeezing his cheeks with his right hand and blowing air from his lungs. Ethan recognized the signs. They planned to make him go back, so he held the dog's restraint loosely to allow him to escape.

"Listen, we talked it over, and only law enforcement can be up here now that homicide is involved. The crime scene unit needs to come up and cordon off this entire area," Barnes said.
"No. We can find her. We found something the others didn't, and Ashley needs me," he said in a firm, stubborn tone.

Barnes gazed at Mills, who shook her head. When he turned back around, Ruger yanked the lead from Ethan's hand and took off running again, just like he hoped he would.

"Shit, Ruger!" Ethan shouted as he chased after him.
"Ethan, wait," Barnes said, chasing after him.

Ruger sprinted through a valley across rocky terrain until he reached a steep rock face. He sniffed the ground and paced as he peered up. Ethan stood beside him and gave him the command.

"Where's mommy, Ruger? Find mommy," he said.

The dog ran along the bottom of the cliff for several feet, stopped, backed up, and barked. Ethan took a few steps back and squinted at the twenty-foot ledge over their heads as Barnes came up behind him. The landscaping is treacherous and steep. They walked around along the side, looking for an easier way up, but there wasn't one.

"We must go back and wait for more agents. A killer is on the loose, and we are chasing a damn canine through the freaking mountains," Barnes said as he huffed.

"Shhh… listen," Ethan insisted, putting his hand up and silencing the agent.

They stood still and concentrated on listening. Quiet humming echoed softly from high above them. Ruger cocked his head and whimpered up at the mountain. Ethan exchanged glances with Barnes, who grabbed his radio as Ethan pulled out his climbing gear and prepared to make the ascent. The steep slope and crumbling surface made finding sturdy crevices to lodge their pitons in challenging. Ruger panted behind Ethan as he made the tiring climb with his hundred-something-pound dog on his back. Barnes reached the ledge first and waited.

The cave entrance is narrow but leads somewhere as they feel a breeze and stale air emanating from its depths. He removed Ruger's harness from his chest and unhooked his leash. Ruger took off through the mountain crack as soon as he became free and didn't return. Barnes radioed the others, telling them their new location before he entered the blacked-out tunnel alone.

Chapter Seven-Free

Someone is coming, but it isn't him. They're approaching from the other side, opposite the waterfall. He's never come from that direction before.

Careful footsteps crunched, barely audible, in the sand, becoming louder as they approached me. Frozen, trapped, and not knowing what to do, I remained silent.

A dark creature sprinted towards me. I shut my eyes, bracing for impact as the animal dove onto me and whined. Ruger's soft hair felt sleek on my cheek as he pushed me with his face, but I couldn't get up. He licked me as though he sensed what I needed and presented it as a gift of affection to ease my sorrow. Then, he leaned into my body and waited.

My dog is here, which means Ethan can't be far behind. I didn't want him to see me like this, and I didn't want the man who took me to kill him.

A silhouette materialized in the shadows, and Ruger snarled an unsettling, throaty growl, warning the intruder to stay back. As the stranger made his way into the light, my teeth chattered, and I shook violently.

The man's gun swept the room from side to side, and his bright green climbing gear practically glowed in the dark. As he closed the gap between us, Ruger became more aggressive.

"Ashley, my name is Agent Barnes. Is anyone else in here?"

Words stuck in my throat, and I choked on them like a steak lodged in my windpipe from not being chewed properly. Nothing came out when I tried to speak. Barnes lowered his weapon when he finished his sweep and tried to come near me, but Ruger lunged at him, forcing him back.

"All right, buddy. I'm here to help remember," he said as the dog bared his fangs. "Ethan, come in here and control this dog, please." The agent hollered behind him.

Ethan sprinted into the room and headed right for me, but I cringed and scooted myself away. He stared at me funny and tried to put his hand on me, but I didn't want to be touched.

"Ashley, it's me… it's Ethan."

He grabbed me and drew me in as I screamed. A female agent ran to our side and pulled Ethan away. He fought against her, not wanting to leave me, and not understanding why she wanted him to go.

"Ethan, take the dog out and wait for me. Barnes, please give us a minute as well."
"No, I want to stay with her," Ethan pleaded with a distressed face.

"I understand, Ethan, but what she needs right now is to feel safe."

The rejection of Ethan's touch devastated me, and I don't know why I reacted to him that way. I have always trusted him, yet the man who took me changed me. Not knowing who or where he could be made me afraid of every man, not just him, and it's not fair, especially to Ethan. Seeing the other official lead Ethan and my pup away from me broke my heart.

Once out of sight, I stared at the bones beside me and thought about my kidnapper. The man said he would never let me go and planned on keeping me. What would he do now that they are taking me away?

My worst fear of anyone finding me naked came true. Multiple people have seen me bare, messy, and battered. If I could have kept it a secret forever, I would have, but I can't hide it now.

The female agent approached and sat before the skeleton, blocking it from me. She reached up and unbuckled my hands from their restraints without touching me. I curled into myself, tucked my palms between my legs, and sobbed. I was free, but not really.

"Hi, Ashley, I'm Agent Mills. I can't imagine what you are going through, and I am sorry, but I need to send in paramedics," she explained.

63

Peering over my shoulder, I drew her attention to the hanging corpses. Mills stood, walked over to them, and then turned to the one still attached to the wall. Kneeling in front of it, she reached over and spun the bracelet on its wrist. The bony hand fell out of the cuff that held it there for so long. She rotated her focus back on me and sighed.

Padding footsteps approached us, and she jumped to her feet. She pulled her gun out and trained it on the opposing entrance near the falls. I grabbed her pant leg and pleaded with my eyes for her not to leave me.

"That's the mountain man," I whispered to her.

Mills stepped further away, removed the safety from her pistol, and prepared to fire. The figure's outline showed itself, but she didn't have a clear view or shot and couldn't just shoot into the dark.

"FBI, don't move."

The person stopped moving at once and retreated but said nothing. She walked closer to the figure and beamed her flashlight at him.

"It's Oliver, ma'am, the ranger."
"Dammit, Oliver, go back to the other end of the tunnel and wait," she said.
"I'm just here to say that we couldn't land the chopper on the other ridge. It's too shallow. They set

down at the bottom of the falls near the clearing at this end," he explained.

"Go back out, and I can call the paramedics when I'm ready, but right now, please go," Mills said.

"Yes, ma'am," Oliver said, turning and retreating down the hollow space.

She returned to my side, sat down, and offered me her hand, which I clutched. Having her with me brought me hope as I picked a white fuzzy off her navy-blue sleeve.

Her shiny black footwear reminded me of one of my old high school teachers. He always wore the most outrageous three-piece suits, and shoes shined to perfection. One day he came in wearing an entirely yellow outfit that resembled a banana. Everyone picked on him, but I loved his bravery. Mills squeezed my hand to get my attention.

"The paramedics need to come in with a backboard for transport. Now, I can go, but Ethan can't. Is that all right?" Mills asked.

I needed to escape this cave with them, but more people would know what happened to me. I may have survived the serial killer, but how can I survive the aftermath?

I want to go home, but I am afraid of my future beyond these walls.

Fatigue took over my body like a blood transfusion. Except, instead of replacing the blood, it drained away. The decision about who rides with me shouldn't be this hard, yet I am torn between hurting Ethan's feelings and being more comfortable with Mills.

I wish they would take me to a hotel and let me be alone. The prying eyes of strangers waiting for me at the hospital and being surrounded by them may worsen things. My head throbbed, and the tension behind my eyes grew uncomfortable. Something dripped from between my legs, but I kept that to myself. A complete exam is in my future, and I am not looking forward to it.

The man didn't use a condom for our encounters, so I prayed he did not give me a deadly disease. Ethan and I always used protection. The thought of someone else's fluids inside me not only grossed me out, but the idea of catching something haunted me even more. So, when we met, I made it clear to Ethan that he always needed to wear one.

I should have fought harder. I should have thrashed about, kicking, and screaming, but then I may have ended up like the others. Perhaps it would have been less complicated and easier for both of us. What happens next may be much more difficult for us than even Ethan can handle. The fact that a stranger deposited his untested liquids inside me made me squirm.

The ground beneath me is comfortable now. Maybe it is because I have weakness from all the trauma. I wonder if the murderer is watching from afar. Seeing the FBI raid his lair and seize his trophies, he's probably infuriated, and I'm to blame—my dog and me. If I am given the possibility of protective custody, Ruger is coming with me.

My stomach rumbled, and Mills placed her hand on my arm. I fell into her kind eyes and trusted her to protect me.

"Please take me out of here."
"Of course," she said, placing her hand on my forehead. "You're safe now."

Chapter Eight-Flowers

The lady paramedic strapped me down to the backboard with the help of Agent Mills. No man could touch me, and everybody completely understood except Ethan.

He grew increasingly frustrated with me, and I can't blame him. It's not his fault; it's the mountain man's. Not letting me see his face made me suspect everyone, even him. Being tied down, blinded, raped, and gagged for the better part of a week caused paranoia, and I took it out on every male who came near me. The waterfall proved to be quite a challenge getting by without soaking us. They covered me with a tarp and tilted the backboard to the side.
After carrying me to the cliff edge, gear waited to lower me down to the waiting chopper stationed at the base of the falls.
As they brought me down slowly, I closed my eyes when the mist floated onto my face and inhaled fresh oxygen. I missed the air, the sky, and the fall scent, taking it for granted. Of the four seasons, this one is my favorite.
The beautiful trees changing from green to unique shades of red, orange, and yellow, begin to die off before winter forces them into hibernation. It is what drew me here to this place.
Agent Mills made sure she scaled down first and met me at the bottom. She gave the crew specific

instructions to avoid handling me. The same instructions were relayed to the health center. Only the female doctor who is on call can be involved.

Once we lifted off, I peered at the other side of the mountain where Ruger and Ethan stood with Oliver and a few other agents. FBI, state police, and park rangers littered the mountainside like ants far below as they labored their way to the homicide scene.

What a beautiful view I have from high above the trees.

The red, orange, and yellow colors would have made a great picture from this elevation. Sadly, I won't return to this lovely place. Death, malicious actions, and unspeakable memories have tarnished it.

When we arrived at the hospital, a woman physician waited for me per Mills request. The bright lights flickered by me as we traveled down a long hallway to a waiting exam room. A woman investigator stood by the door to my room with a bag to secure evidence. I'm unsure what she planned to collect from me. I'm naked.

"Hi Ashley, I'm Detective Folwell, and I'm here to take samples."

"Can't we do it later?" I asked.

"Unfortunately, no. I promise my part is not that difficult. I need to scrape underneath every fingernail, comb hair from both the head and pubis, and swab some skin surfaces. The doc needs to do the internal exam and give me the specimens afterward. I can stay in the room, or I can go if you're more comfortable," she said.

Without answering, I put my hand out so she could take her sample and leave me be. She scraped so deep under my nails that she extended their length, and when she combed out my snarled hair, she took a few by the roots as well.
The gynecologist came in with a kit and sat at the end of the bed. I tightened my limbs together like a vise, reddening my knees. Mills came into the room, and the detective stepped out. She sat beside me in a faux leather chair with no arms and took my hand.

"This may be difficult, but it must be done. I'm right here. Focus on me," she said.

I nodded at her and tried to keep my attention on her face, but I couldn't relax enough to be touched between the legs.

"Ashley, look at me. Take a deep breath in, and then when you let it out, allow the legs to fall open," the doctor said. "Shout, cry, or scream, if needed. Whatever it takes."

My eyes filled with tears that spilled down my face as I inhaled deeply and exhaled. When I felt her, my bottom flew off the table as I screamed.

Mill's face cringed as I crushed her hand, fighting against the doctor's touch. The monitors beside me sounded the alarm on my blood pressure and pulse as they skyrocketed to dangerous levels.

The doctor stopped the examination at once and gave me a sedative. It melted through my veins and drained the life out of my body. Mills rubbed my head tenderly as I drifted into a deep, needed sleep.

Flower arrangements surrounded me when I woke up. Their soft petals should have been welcoming, but not for me. Their floral vapors set off my gag reflex, and I dry heaved. Ethan jumped up from the chair beside me, startling me.

"What? What is it? What can I do?"
"No flowers. Please take them away."

He snatched them two at a time and took them to the nurse's desk. The nurse came into the room objecting to her sudden full counter and lack of workspace.

"These floral arrangements are not mine. They need to stay in this room," the nurse snarled, bringing one back in.

The nurse made a mistake when she set the flowers next to me. I am already in a delicate frame of mind, so pressing me was not in her best interest, which she soon learned as I launched the flowers out of my room.

They shattered on the front side of her post and made a massive mess on the floor. Mills stood next to the fractured vase, watched a petal slide down the front of the nurse's station in slow motion, and entered my room.

"What is the issue with the flowers?" Mills asked.

I didn't want Ethan to know every seductive thing the man did to me inside the cave, so I didn't reply. I know he meant well when he bought me a dozen roses, but I couldn't stand their presence. All the blooms must go.

"Ashley?" Ethan touched my arm, and I jolted away.

He sighed, sat in his chair, and Mills settled on my other side. She held the notes from people who brought the arrangements in her hand. They checked every one of them as they came in to see if any came from the killer. She handed them to me, but I didn't want to see them, so she gave them to Ethan.
Most came from coworkers, family, strangers, and friends, but one particularly struck me as weird. When Ethan read it, the hair on my arm stood attention, and my skin crawled like a thousand spiders running across it.
"Reread it," I said to Ethan.

"The same one?"
"Yes. Read it again, please."

Ashley,

I'd like us to continue working together when the time is right. I want to keep you. There is no way I could ever let you go.

Attorney Johnston

What an odd thing to say to someone he treats as though he hates on most days. Why did he send me flowers? And, more importantly, how did they get here?

"Ethan, did he bring these here?"
"The aide brought them in, but I can ask her how they got here."

When he left the room, Mills turned to me. "What is it?"
"When the man spoke to me in the cave, he said he would keep me and never let me go. It seemed similar, but it's my boss, of all people. He's an asshole, not a serial killer," I said nervously. "Right?"

Mills placed her hand on my shoulder and stepped out of the room. I have a feeling that my boss just became the target of the investigation though I doubted his involvement. Ethan's elevated voice echoed through the hall outside my room shortly after. When I tried to stand up to see, I fell to the floor. The drugs the doctor gave me made my muscles like noodles.

I fumbled about, trying to find my bearings, but my head bounced about, my eyes declined to focus, and I fell back over, taking my side table with me. It smashed against the wall, spilling water everywhere.

The nurse, Ethan, and Mills flooded the room and nearly slipped on my mess. Ethan ran to me and gripped me from behind, but I started shouting at him, so he put his hands up and backed away. The nurse hoisted me up with the aid of Mills and helped me back into bed.

"Next time, use the call switch. That's what it's for," she said, stuffing it in my hand.

Ethan sat at the end of the mattress instead of the chair and stared at me. I didn't know what to say to him. He eventually would find out everything that happened, but I was just not ready to tell my story to him. Mill's phone rang, and she excused herself from taking the call.

"What were you yelling about?"
"Ashley, nothing has changed between us. I'm here to talk to no matter what, as long as it takes. Trust me, please."

"Answer the question, Ethan."
"The agent won't tell me what happened to you," he said.
"I'm not ready."
"I understand. We can take it day by day, but I wish you could trust me enough to confide in me. I love you," he said.

Crying isn't a proper response to what he said, but how can he still love me after what happened? I don't even love myself. I know he has strong suspicions about what occurred during my captivity.

Even if I bleached my body inside and out, I would still feel dirty. The man who kidnapped me took more from me in that cave than my soul. He took my love of flowers, my want for intimacy, my need for attention, and most of all, my ability to trust any man away from me. Until he's caught, I may never be free from this nightmare.

Chapter Nine-The Interview

The night shift aide introduced herself as Doris. Her striking white hair, trim build, and how she sped around my room reminded me of my grandmother. Her firm but cheery demeanor and dry humor brought a spark into the dismal, outdated room.

She snatched my water pitcher, put it to her nose, and sniffed it for cleanliness. By her expression, it didn't meet her standards, and she quickly took it out of the room and returned with a new one. She seized a paper cup, filled it with crushed ice and water, and gave it to me.

"Drink up. A fit girl with a high metabolism needs several healthy meals and a lot of water," she said, with a perfectly white dentured smile.
"Thanks for being so kind. The morning lady is so mean."
"She's a bitch. No need to sugarcoat it. These young women today think they are special. They have all this fancy equipment to do stuff now. But let that power go out, and we have to do things the old way by hand, and they are useless," she smiled, patting me on the shoulder.

I returned the favor, smirked, and then put my water down without a sip. She stood in front of my bed and waited, saying nothing. Her piercing blue eyes and pursed lips told me she wouldn't leave until I drank my water, so I quickly grabbed it and sucked it down.

"Excellent work," she said, grabbing my empty paper cup and refilling it for the next time.

She typed some notes on the computer before speed-walking back out of the room. Agent Mills sat in a chair outside, waiting for the DNA results from the crime scene.

They had identified the dismembered hiker from a missing person's report but never found his clothes. Either the killer stashed them or destroyed them.

Ethan left a long time ago to grab something to eat. Having the room all to myself made my stay more tolerable, and visiting hours are ending soon. No one can stay the night, hospital rules. The only exception is for ICU patients, which I am not. Perhaps he didn't want to return. I wouldn't blame him.

Look what I have done, what the mountain man did. I didn't want him here, but I didn't want him to leave me. Confusion and heartache ripped me apart inside as I struggled with my feelings.

A patient kitty corner from me by the nurse's station screamed for her beer. Apparently, she gets a brewski at dinnertime, and they forgot to send it. Her infernal yelling made my head throb, and I would do anything to shut her up, so I pressed my call button to summon Doris.

"Yes, Ashley," Doris said.

"Tylenol for me and an alcoholic beverage for her," I replied.

"Sorry about her. She can be noisy sometimes. At least you're getting out of here tomorrow," she said as she left the room.

Tomorrow...

Where can I go that's safe? The man from the mountains took my driver's license. He knows where I live, and searching my name online would tell him where I work, so neither of those places is secure.

Agent Mills arrived and stood at the foot of my bed. She leaned onto the handrail and exhaled, inflating her cheeks. When she made eye contact, their disappointment gave me the news before it passed her lips.

"Initial DNA results have yielded no suspects. Everything they have found thus far has been transferred from all of us that came into the cave after," she said, placing her hands on the rail.

"And the women?"

"We are still identifying the bodies."

I rolled onto my side and stared out of my room. He kept me for all those days and did so many things to me but left no trace of himself. How is that possible?

Mills came and sat in the chair before me, forcing me to acknowledge her presence.

"It's time to tell me everything. It could help us with the investigation."

A single tear made a short journey down my face and dropped on my pillow. I don't want to talk about it, but she won't let it go until I do, so I told her. Every horrible moment, detail, my inappropriate responses, what he said to me, everything. She recorded it on her phone, so she didn't miss a thing. By the time I finished, she seemed disgusted.

I curled myself into a ball and cried all my humiliation out into the open. She tried to reassure me that my feelings were normal for my situation, but it didn't make a difference. The filth I am now stained with can never be cleansed.

Under the circumstances, they decided it would be best for me to stay at a hotel for a few days before returning home. Because the killer took my fanny pack with identification inside, they wanted me in protective custody.

Ruger would sleep with me at the hotel, but not Ethan, which crushed him. We bickered back and forth about it until we finally reached a compromise. He would stay in a separate adjoining room with the door open in case I needed him. That way, he's out of sight but nearby if I change my mind.

Doris gave me a sleeping pill to help me rest through the night, and it worked, maybe a little too well. I slept for twelve hours and woke up having to pee so badly that I thought my bladder might rupture. It came out like a faucet on full blast and didn't stop for almost a minute.

"Good lord, Ashley," Doris said, raising her penciled eyebrows when I retreated from the restroom.
"What are you still doing here?"
"The morning nurse is coming in later," she said. "Hungry?"
"Starving."
"Well, breakfast is over, but lunch is arriving soon. Unfortunately, it's too late to choose from the menu, so whatever comes is it. But I can make peanut butter and jelly if it's too gross."
"Sounds good."

She left after helping me back to bed. Later this afternoon, they are driving me to a hotel to stay the night. I couldn't wait to see Ruger. He saved my life, and I wanted to reward him with extra love.
Ethan came into the room and sat in a corner chair. Something is on his mind, but he is keeping it to himself. Doris returned after a few minutes with my lunch. She placed it on my side table, adjusted its height, and slid it in front of me. The turkey sandwich appeared edible as I scanned my tray and stopped.
Fear gripped my throat and pierced through my eyes as the cup of chocolate pudding on the edge of

81

my tray triggered a violent response from inside me. My hands instinctively shot the surface away from me, and it crashed to the floor as my arms quaked like the San Andreas fault. My head split right down the middle and fractured as I screamed until my throat went raw.

Multiple nurses and a doctor appeared in the doorway, but Doris raised her hand to stop them from entering. Ethan had jumped from his chair, and Doris stared in shock with a chest full of food as I shook violently with chattering teeth. My insides rumbled like thunder, and I ran to the toilet to empty my bowels. Adrenaline took all my pain away and gave me the strength to express my emotions like never before.

"Ashley, what can I do to help," Ethan asked outside the bathroom door.

"Don't come in here."

"I'm not. Doris said she's getting something for the anxiety," he said through the door.

Of all the things to bring me for a lunchtime snack, they chose chocolate pudding. Surely it was just a coincidence, but my mind refused to see it that way.

"Ashley, it's Doris. The mess has been cleaned, and I brought a pill for the panic attacks," she said as she tapped on the door.

"Just another minute," I said to her.

Several minutes would be better. My vile intestinal contents stunk up the space like a sewage intake facility. My fumes now contaminate its once clean white walls and sterile tiles. I flushed, washed my hands, climbed into the shower, gown and all, and turned it on hot.

My skin reddened instantly as the stinging fire spray burned me, but I didn't move. The door shuttered rapidly as Ethan pounded on the other side, but I didn't stir. I sat there, letting my sinful body burn, hoping it would wash my shame away like holy water at church on Sunday.

Chapter Ten-Scolded

Ethan burst into the bathroom with Doris, who turned the water to cool. My lobster-red, angry skin no longer felt the heat, and my tears washed down the drain like the rest of my life.

Ethan stood silent with his mouth gapped open, seeing all my visible bruises of various shapes, sizes, and colors for the first time. They littered my flesh with fierce shades of green, blue, brown, and purple. All of which told a story I had no intention of sharing with him.

Easily being bruised is something I have dealt with my whole life, so all the man-handling and dangling from the cave ceiling did a number on my wrists and ankles. My cheek wore a shadow of its own, compliments of my defiance to sing and my kidnapper's sizeable hand.

Doris pushed Ethan out of the restroom, closed the door, and gingerly removed my gown.

"Ashley, why are you doing this?"
"No matter how much I wash, I'm still dirty."

She yanked a nearby towel from its bar, turned the water off, and gently patted my skin.

"Ashley, this is all normal behavior for someone who has been through this type of crime. I have a business card for a counselor specializing in trauma. Call her anytime."

I don't want to talk, I want to forget, but everyone keeps bringing it up. Keeping things locked up inside isn't healthy, but I wanted to keep things where they were safe.

Doris took me by the elbow and helped me out of the shower. Ethan brought a pair of gray sweatpants, a T-shirt, socks, a bra, and underwear and set them outside the door so I could get dressed. A pen and notepad sat on my table beside the bed when I came out.

"Mills, what's this?"

"Write the triggers we need to avoid. Food, items, phrases, anything that may cause an anxiety attack."

My hand hesitated when I took the writing utensil. Ethan eyed me intently, waiting for me to begin. I'm not sure how much more disappointment I can take. When I wrote the last thing that may trigger, Ethan sighed, and left the room.

I never meant to hurt him, but they needed a complete list, so I gave it to them. Ethan fell into the last category, men.

Mills walked out of the room after him, so I sat on my bed alone, and stared at the floor. Its shiny tile and speckled pattern drew me to it, and my eyes got stuck. The ringing in my ears began slowly and rose to intolerable levels. It went from one to the other and disappeared as fast as it came. Doris's fingers snapped in front of my face, bringing me back to earth.

"Ashley, is everything all right?"

I laid back, turned away from her, and remained soundless. What a stupid question. Before too long, she carried in my discharge paperwork, and two officers joined Mills in the hall. The officers will escort us to the motel, then stay outside my room in the hall on rotating shifts.

A squeaky wheelchair rolled through the door to take me to the lobby. We sat stagnant while Ethan drove the car around, and Mills waited by my side. The hospital's exterior crawled with reporters, all wanting the first glimpse of the woman who survived the Cavern Killer. That's what they have named him. How original. Doris ran up behind us before we left and handed me the card for the counselor.

"Here's a blanket. Don't let those vultures take a single picture. They only care about the story and not people's feelings," she said.

"Thanks," I said, squishing her hand on my shoulder.

Mills took the blanket and partially covered me and the wheelchair as the police cleared a path to our car. The cover shielded me until Ethan gave us the all-clear. The mountains appeared before us, and

I clutched the back of Mill's seat so tightly that my fingernails bent backward. My heartbeat thumped inside my head and pounded against my chest.

"Ethan, don't go this way," I insisted.
"But this is the way to the hotel."
"Find another way," I shrieked at him with balled-up fists.

Ethan turned the wheel sharply and took a bunch of side streets to get us to the hotel's back parking lot. I forgot to add mountains to the list. It should have been obvious, but maybe not to them. Screaming is very out of character for me. I'm usually level-headed, but my moods have been so touchy lately, and I don't like it.

"Sorry, I yelled," I said to Ethan's reflection.
"It's okay," he replied.

I leaned against the window and waited for Ethan to check us in before exiting. A young couple unloaded their car while their children argued over whose turn it was to play on the iPad. The boys yanked it back and forth between them, almost dropping it multiple times. Their mother took the decision away by placing it in the outside pocket of her leopard print luggage.

The hotel lobby bustled with people, and their closeness plucked my last nerve as I did my best to avoid them. The sitting area carpet is velvety red with paisley gold wingback chairs and a stone fireplace to keep guests warm. It seemed like a pleasant place to read a book.

Every man that passed by me and peered in my direction, I thought, is it him? I drew my arms against my body to protect myself from their prying eyes.

Our room is on the top floor with a dull parking lot view. Most people chose the other side, but they knew better now. Each of us has a king-size bed in our adjoining rooms, and the officers swept our room before retreating into the hall with Mills.

"I need to pick up Ruger from the boarding place down the road. I'll be back soon," Ethan said, grabbing the keys from the counter.

When he stepped toward me, I shied away, so he spun the keys on his finger, turned, and left. I flipped on the television in my room and lay down. The plush mattress welcomed my tired body, and my stomach growled, so I grabbed the room service menu. Nothing sounded appetizing, but I needed to eat something. I settled on a side salad and a cup of minestrone with a dinner roll.

The officer outside my room checked the food when it arrived and compared it to my list. She removed the flower from the vase in the middle and rolled it into me. After only eating a bite of a tomato and a couple of spoons of soup, my appetite disappeared. I took the roll off my cart to save for

Ruger and wheeled it back to the door for the officer.

Ethan didn't return until nightfall with Ruger. His nub wiggled back and forth when he entered my room and jumped on the bed. He made himself comfortable and ate the bread I kept for him. I petted his smooth black and rusty coat as he licked the crumbs off the white duvet.

"He missed you," Ethan said, standing in the doorway between our rooms.

"I missed him too."

Our eyes locked, and I thought he might say something more, but he smiled, adjusted his wire-rimmed glasses, and walked away. He's giving me my space, and I appreciate it. Still, his presence made me feel on edge despite dating for so long. I took my pillow, stuffed it securely between my legs, and laid down. Ruger cuddled up to me, and we fell asleep listening to a meteorologist talk about a storm rolling in.

Chapter Eleven-The Storm

Thunder cracked and rattled the walls, awakening me. I turned over to face the window and view the lightning. The tall silhouette of a man flashed before me as rain fell against the window.

I flailed my arms, tumbled out of bed, and ran screaming to the adjoining space with Ruger on my heels. The officer met me at the door with her gun drawn and shielded me with her body. Ruger stood between the unknown intruder and us. The unsettled air dissipated at once when Ethan's voice pierced the silence in the dark.

"It's just me. I'm sorry. I didn't mean to scare you," he said, coming into the light with his hands up.

His camera hung ready for use from his neck, and his rain jacket dripped water onto the carpet. The officer put her weapon away, sighed, and returned to the hallway.

"Ethan, what the hell are you doing?" I asked in a shaking voice.
"After I went out to take pictures of the storm, I came in to check on you. You and Ruger were spooning, so I took a picture."
"Let me see," I demanded.

He removed the camera and gave it to me. I seemed so peaceful and content in the perfectly captured image. Now I understand why he took it. The other photos are from when the storm first rolled in. Several were of cloud-to-ground lightning and the mountains lighting up like daytime as the torrential downpour began.

"Ethan, you scared me," I said, wiping a tear from my cheek.
"I'm sorry. It won't happen again. Why can't I sleep in here with you? The bed is enormous. I can stay on one side and you on the other. Ruger always lays in the middle anyway," he pleaded.
"I'm sorry," I said, as the tears changed from drips to falls.

He took his equipment from me and moved aside so I may retire to my room. I curled up and cried to myself with my dog next to me. He's the only male I trust now, and he's not human.
The alarm clock blinked red numbers at me when I opened my eyes. The storm took power with it when it charged through town overnight, but the electric company restored it before dawn. I glanced outside, and downed branches and debris littered the parking lot's surface. Employees moved through the lot, picking up the mess and putting it in the back of a pickup truck.
I turned on the television and watched the news. A reporter started talking about the damage the

weather caused throughout our area. I turned it off and took a hot shower. I have been here for two days, and this is my fourth shower.

My dry, flaky skin felt the brunt of my new obsession with being clean, so I smeared a large amount of lotion all over me. I stood there staring at myself in the mirror and burst into tears. It's the lotion. I can't take the feel of it on my body. I climbed back in the shower and scrubbed it off, returning my skin to its crusty self.

The squeaky wheel of a cart approached my room, and the officer appeared with my breakfast. Ethan must have taken Ruger for a walk. They are both gone. I removed the lid on my food, and a Belgian waffle and oatmeal stared back at me.

The golden circle looked overdone, but it tasted soft and delicious in my mouth. After consuming the entire confection, I sucked down a whole cup of coffee. I had an appetite for the first time in a long time, so I enjoyed it while it lasted.

I grabbed Ethan's camera from the table in his room and swiped through its contents. The number of pictures he continued to take despite my peril astonished me.

When we met, he told me about his unhealthy attachment to cameras. He had all different kinds, from digital to film, and our daily conversations often drifted toward comparing the benefits and downfalls of each type. Never in my life would I have imagined he would still take pictures after I disappeared. For someone who says he loves me, he loves his cameras more.

He came in with Ruger, and I set the camera aside. I made a decision that Ethan won't like, but I need to think about myself for once.

"Ethan, you need to go home."

"Ashley, what are you talking about?"

"I don't think you want to be here, so I want you to go. I understand if you need to take the dog until I check out of the hotel, but I prefer him to stay."

"I want to stay here, please. Why are you doing this? I can protect you."

"Leave now," I yelled, drawing the officer into the room.

"What's the problem?" She asked.

"Nothing. Ethan is leaving. Right now," I told her.

"Ashley, don't leave me. I love you."

"I'm not leaving you. You left me," I replied.

I took his camera and handed it to him without saying another word, then walked over to my side. He came toward me as I closed the door and locked him out.

His infernal knocking became so loud that I covered my head with a pillow and turned up the television. He puts me second in his life all the time. I don't know where my bravery came from, but I am glad it did. I need to let him go.

Perhaps it isn't bravery at all? It may just be an excuse to kick him out of my life for good, even if it has nothing to do with him. I don't want him to be stuck with damaged goods. He's too gentle. He needs someone stronger, more tolerable, someone clean, not me. I'm nothing more than a piece of tarnished flatware that belongs in a drawer somewhere so I can be long forgotten.

   I longed to be free. Free to hide, stay quiet, walk out of this hotel, and not give a shit who may or may not be following me. But I can't even leave this room without worrying that the first man I run into might be the Cavern Killer returning to finish the job.

   The doorknob to my room turned itself downward, and Mills came inside. She walked over to the window and sat down on the sill. I'm sure Ethan told her I kicked him out.

"We have identified all the women. Some women who fit the description are still missing, but they may have nothing to do with this. Ethan left Ruger for you. He's lying on the bed in the other room. He said to tell you he loves you and that he's sorry," Mills said.

   He can be sorry all he wants, but after what I've been through, I am in no position or state of mind to tolerate indifference. He should have put my safety and feelings first, not his stupid camera or desire to photograph nature at its best. What happened to me changed my perspective on life.

I have more important things to worry about, like going home alone when they still haven't found the man who hurt me. At least I have Ruger for protection. Ethan and I never moved in together. We stayed at each other's places. He never asked, and I never offered, but Ruger is my dog, despite our co-training and mutual love for him. He is staying with me when I leave this temporary hideaway.

I can never go back to work, even though my boss offered for me to return when I am ready. Being in the public eye for court cases and involved in the legal system carries too much exposure. I don't want anyone to lose focus on the job or be unable to speak freely for fear that they may trigger a painful memory. I need a different place of employment and a new apartment to live in.

Moving out of town seemed like a practical choice. Somewhere with no view of the mountains everywhere I go. The ocean might be lovely, as I have always loved the beach. The problem is that the sand would constantly remind me of the cave the mountain man held me captive in and the dead rib my toes touched.

So, where does that leave me? Where could I move to that doesn't have mountains, sand, flowers, and life? If I changed my name and dyed my hair differently, no one would recognize me, not even the killer. But what is the point of living if I must erase my identity?

I have lost everything, including my will to survive. Hopeless and afraid, I grabbed a handful of sleeping pills from the doctor's bottle, threw them down my throat, and went to bed.

Chapter Twelve-A Secret Worth Keeping

Noisy monitors chirped around me, and a light shined into my eyes, making me wince. As much as I hated hospitals, what I did landed me right back inside one.

I wanted to take more than enough to forget but not enough to take my life. A thin line exists between the two, and I tipped too far over to the wrong side.

A doctor stood next to me and put his hand on mine. I flinched away from him, and he took a step away. My eyes blurred a bit, and I opened and closed them while shaking my head back and forth, trying to clear the clutter.

"Welcome back, Ashley."

My vitals jumped to dangerous levels, and I began hyperventilating after he touched me again. My eyes widened, darting around the room, looking for a way out. The doctor came to my side and attempted to calm me. A third touch is all it took for my fight or flight to engage. I swung at the physician, striking him multiple times when he touched my leg. Mills ran into the room and grabbed ahold of me from behind.

"Ashley, stop. This is Dr. Furley."

I pushed her away and fell to the floor in complete despair. Mills took Dr. Furley outside to have a private word with him while the aide on duty came to my side. She didn't talk. She just listened to me sob as I tried to pull myself together. What a mess I have become and continue to be.

The cold hard tiles stung my knees when I landed, and I rubbed them with force. It reminded me of the killer warming me by the fire, so I stopped at once. My hands curled into themselves to prevent them from touching me. Dr. Furley returned to the room but kept his distance.

"Ashley, I apologize. Now that I understand the circumstances behind your reaction, we need to discuss a few things, no more sleeping pills. Over-the-counter sleep aids, chamomile tea, and meditation are fine, but no more prescriptions. The next thing we need to talk about is a bit more sensitive," he said, gesturing for the aide to leave with his head.

She stepped out of the room, leaving us alone. I glanced at the door, looking for Mills, but she didn't come in. I backed up as far away from him as the wall would allow so that he couldn't reach me. He kneeled before me, took a pen from his chest pocket, and circled something on paper.

"These test results came in this morning."

The doctor slid the clipboard across the floor in my direction, and I picked it up. One test caught my attention thanks to the doctor's blue ink. My eyes got stuck on the page as my brain blacked out temporarily. I quivered violently as the memory of my sexual assault returned. A dribble of phantom bodily fluids belonging to the mountain man drained down my thigh. The paper crushed under my grip as I reread the test results.

Pregnancy-result positive

The clipboard fell out of my hand and tumbled to the ground. The doctor reached over, retrieved it, and uncrumpled the paper. My head spun, and the room moved around me like the moon orbiting the earth as I absorbed the news. Everything inside me changed in an instant when I read those results. My hands shook, and I wept heavily as I realized who the father must be.

The mountain man took so much from me but left a part of himself as a parting gift, his child.

Vomit surged into my throat and tossed out of my mouth like a long, silent volcano. The doctor jumped away to avoid the half-digested contents of my stomach. The liquid flowed away from me like lava moving through a valley as it spread across the floor.

"Now, options are available. It's early enough to start a regimen to take care of it," he explained.

"Like an abortion? No, it's a baby, not an 'it.' I can't kill her for something that's not her fault," I cried.

"Her?"

He stood up when I didn't respond and left the room, making no attempt to clean up the mess. A few minutes later, the aide returned with a yellow bucket on wheels and started mopping up my biohazard. The contents of my belly smeared around the floor, filled with chunks and slime, and my mouth watered. I crawled several feet to the bathroom and vomited in the toilet.

The heaving turned so violent that I thought I might break a rib. The porcelain became my headrest as I waited for the next round of vile liquid to reach the surface.

When nothing happened, I moved away from the toilet and rested my head on the wall near the red call button. The string swayed back and forth, taunting me. I thought about pulling the rope, but finding out I was pregnant by my rapist wasn't a medical emergency.

Mills stood at the bathroom door with her hand over her nose. I don't understand why she is still here. Perhaps she thinks I'm her best lead because she has been on this case for so long trying to apprehend this killer. Or maybe I am the bait, just a dirty worm for her to use to catch the biggest fish of her career.

"What did the doctor have to say?"

"Nothing. Can I go home?" I asked.

"Well, we can return to the hotel tomorrow. Ethan came to pick up Ruger and took him to the kennel. He's in the waiting room."

"Now is not the best time," I said, wiping vomit from my chin.

"Don't keep pushing him away. I'm not trying to make excuses for him. He is suffering. Give him five minutes," she said.

"Fine, five minutes, but then come take him out of here."

She smiled and disappeared. I got up, brushed my teeth, and sat in a seat next to my bed. He can't find out my secret. No one can. I picked my lower lip with my thumb and pointer finger while waiting for his arrival. My leg bounced up and down until heavy footsteps stopped outside my door. I gripped the chair seat and dug my fingers into the leather. Ethan peeked around the corner, and I shied away.

"Hi," he said.

The scuff of a shoe on the tile became my focus, and Ethan would have no part in me ignoring him. He got down on the floor and into my line of vision. I didn't want him to see my shame, so I closed my eyes and prayed that when I opened them, he would be gone.

I needed a hot shower as I felt dirtier now than ever, but I needed to wait until he left first, so I sat there, uncomfortable in my skin. Sweat rolled down my spine and landed on my seat as the room heated around me.

"Please, look at me," he pleaded.
"Ethan, I can't do this now."
"Talk to me. Tell me what I can do to make this right?"
"Get rid of the camera," I said, with fire raging in my now open watery eyes.
"My camera? What does my camera have to do with any of this?" he said, elevating his voice and towering over me as he stood.

My upper limbs pulled into my chest as I tucked my pressed-together hands between my legs, shrinking under his tall stature. Mills came in and sensed my discomfort.

"Ethan, it's time to leave."
"I'm not done talking," he said without looking away.
"Want to bet?" she said, stepping in between us and gesturing him to the door.

He sighed, put his hands on his hips, and left the room. Once in the hallway, he turned and glared at me with a darkness I had never seen before.

The hair on the back of my neck elevated, and my skin prickled. My pulse pounded in my neck, and my hands shook. His last words rattled me when they shouldn't have.

"This isn't over," he said, wagging his finger back and forth in the air between us.

Chapter Thirteen-Going Home

After my short stint in the hospital, Mills took me back to the hotel to gather my things. I'm going home, not back to the hotel, not into protective custody, home.

If they want to sit outside my house and babysit me, that's on them. No one will protect my little girl as I will. Little girl, that's what I have in my dreams. My beautiful baby has fiery red hair, a spunky personality, and is smarter than me.
    I'm getting us out of here, packing a small bag, taking my money out in cash, and moving away from this nightmare. Somewhere no one can find us.
    As we came closer to my apartment, I asked Mills to stop at the bank so I could pull out some cash for groceries. Little did she know, I had the rest put into a cashier's check that I secretly tucked into my bra.
    I turned around and joined Mills by the entrance so we could return to the car. When we rounded the corner onto my street, reporters lined the road on both sides, sidewalks, and curbs, talking amongst themselves as they waited for me to show up.

"Keep driving," I said to Mills.
"Having second thoughts?"
"No, take me around the back. There is a gate that no one can get through without a keycard. It's where I usually park."

Mills drove around the block and beeped to clear us a path. Once inside the fence, lights from the reporter's cameras flickered around us as we made our way to the back door of my two-story apartment building. We took the elevator to the upper floor, and I stopped short upon exiting. Mills continued walking, unfazed by Ethan sitting outside my door with Ruger. When she realized I wasn't behind her, she came back to me.

"Ethan's just here to bring Ruger, not to start trouble," she reassured me.

I walked behind her, avoiding his eyes as the distance between us became less and less. He stood up from the floor and waited silently as I took out my key and handed it to Mills. We stood in the hallway with Ruger while Mills checked the place out.

"You look beautiful today," he said.
"Thanks."
"Ashley, I would feel more comfortable if I could stay here, so you're not alone," he said, moving toward me.
"Ruger will be with me," I replied, stepping back.

Mills came out of the apartment before he could say anything more.

"All clear," she said, holding the door for me.

She stepped in Ethan's path when he tried to enter behind me, so he let go of Ruger's leash.

"Remember what we talked about," she said to him.
"This is bullshit," he said as he walked away.

Mills closed the door once she saw him get on the elevator. I could tell she had something on her mind and was having difficulty putting it into words.

"Ashley, we have a person of interest in custody. Now, he claims to have an alibi, but I think he might be the one."
"What? Who is it?"
"One of the rangers that helped with the search. We found him in possession of the broken camera. There are disturbing images on his home computer, and he is also on the sex offender registry," she explained.

A tear went down my cheek and splattered on the hickory laminate flooring. Running off in the night may not happen after all, though it still sounded better than staying here and facing Ethan.
I thanked her before she left to instruct the officers outside my building on their assignment. A fine layer of dust covered all my apartment surfaces, so I snatched a cloth off the counter and cleaned. A

little dusting turned into a total cleanse of the whole place.

Sweat soaked my back, and the hair around my face stuck to my temples, so I grabbed a cozy robe and stepped into the shower. The water felt pleasant as it washed over my body. I rubbed my lower belly and wondered how she was doing in there.

As I dried myself off, I heard the phone ringing in the living room. Since it was probably Ethan, I just ignored it and brushed my teeth. The taste of my toothpaste usually doesn't bother me, but now it feels intolerable. My gums and tongue burned as I scrubbed, so I cut my routine short and rinsed my mouth twice. My little girl is already changing me.

Ruger is on the sofa spread out when I exit the bathroom. His lips fluttered in his sleep, and he made whiney noises as he dreamed. The front door rattled to my left, making me jump and jolting Ruger awake. When I peered through the peephole, my breath caught in my throat at the sight of my boss standing on the other side of the steel divide. I tried to ignore the knocking, but it became more insistent, so I gave in.

"Mr. Johnston, what are you doing here?" I asked through the door.

"Brought some pastries from that restaurant by the office, and I thought we could talk," he said.

"I'm not up for company."

"Please? Five minutes and then I can go," he insisted.

"I'm coming out. Ruger, stay," I said, putting my hand up to him.

Turning my body sideways, I slid into the hallway as Ruger growled a throaty warning to the attorney. I left the door ajar, so he could still see me, but he didn't like not being in between us.

"How did you get in the building?"
"The old lady next door. She left the gate open, and I helped her carry in her groceries," he said, pointing.
"I need to speak with her about that."
"First, I wanted to make sure you were safe. Now that I have seen you, I feel better. The other reason is to see if you would be willing to do paperwork from home. That way you can still have money coming in and help me at the same time. Work is backing up, and this temporary worker they sent me is inefficient," he said, placing his hand on my arm and caressing it with his thumb.

There was a time when Ethan and I started dating that Mr. Johnston asked me out. I would have said yes, but the timing was bad.
After I rejected him, he became less tolerant of my mistakes than others. Perhaps I was reading into it too much and making assumptions. He's here now as though he cares and offering job security, but once again, it's not a good time.

I pulled myself away at once and moved inside my apartment. The attorney followed me, which was not a bright idea, as Ruger jumped between us, with his hair standing on end, baring his teeth.

"Easy, boy. I'm not going to hurt her," he said, backing away from us.

"Please, get out," I insisted.

"Ashley, I'm sorry I didn't mean anything by it. It was not my intention to upset you."

His brown bedroom eyes and playful smile seemed sincere, but that didn't matter. What matters is my level of comfort, and right now, I am not comfortable at all. I'm not sure what happened after that moment, as my eyes went black without warning, and I couldn't see. My legs failed me simultaneously, and I dropped to the floor like a cup falling off the counter, bouncing when I landed. I couldn't talk, move, or see, but I could hear.

"Ashley, what's the matter? Should I call an ambulance? Ashley?"

The attorney's voice echoed far away inside my head, and my mind took me elsewhere as he shook me. Garbled fighting became clear as my eyesight returned long enough to see Ethan punching Attorney Johnson repeatedly before I passed out.

I woke up on the couch with Mills sitting with another woman across from me. The fog in my head lifted enough for me to sit up. My head throbbed, and excessive saliva made its way into my palette before I had an opportunity to speak. I frantically ran to the bathroom, stumbling the entire course, and vomited.

After rinsing my mouth a few times, I returned to the living room.

"Who's this?" I said, pointing at the woman.

"I'm Dr. Reed," she said, smiling softly. "Agent Mills called the hospital and requested a home visit, so that's what I'm here to do."

Mills stood up and walked over to the door, leaving without a word.

"Does she know you're pregnant?" the doctor asked.

"I haven't told anyone."

"Ashley, a drop in blood sugar or pressure most likely caused the fainting spell. Right now, the best thing to do is to take things slow and eat small meals every couple of hours. Also, get some prenatal vitamins and start taking them. Here is the appointment card for the first ultrasound."

"I will. Thanks."

"Take care," she said.

Mills stepped back into the room, sat at the counter, and folded her hands in front of her.

"Ethan is in jail. He put quite a beating on Mr. Johnston, but he's making bail as we speak. Also, we cleared the ranger. His alibi checked out. I'm sorry, he is not our guy."

"So, the man who hurt me is still roaming free somewhere, and we are back to square one. Unbelievable," I said as I paced the room.

"Ashley, why did Mr. Johnston come here?"

"He wants me back to work and brought pastries from my favorite restaurant. I told him I was not ready, then he put his hand on my arm, and I guess I passed out."

"Ethan thought he was trying to hurt you, so that's why he attacked him," Mills said.

"Why did he come back to my apartment? Did he say?"

"He came to bring this," she said, holding up an envelope. "He said he planned to slip it under the door, but when he showed up, the door was ajar, and he heard a man yelling. Well, I have to get back, but next time someone comes to the door, please call me, or flag the officer out front to come. Don't answer it."

Inside my head, I wanted to tell her not to leave me and spill the beans on my situation, but as she walked out the door, I stopped myself. Sneaking away in the middle of the night wouldn't be possible if she decided to stay over.

Between the hospital comment and this fight with my boss, perhaps Mills is right. Ethan is having a difficult time. Maybe I'm wrong for not letting him be around, but I feel it would be too uncomfortable for us both, especially now that I am pregnant.

I stared down at my attire and realized I never got dressed, but it was almost dinner time, so I didn't bother. The plush ivory robe covered most of me, and that's all that mattered as I stood in front of the closet, thinking. If I were to go, what essentials would I need to take?

Comfortable clothes are necessary in the future, and the same goes for shoes. No more heels for me. I need practicality. Fancy dresses are unnecessary, and skinny jeans would only be wearable for a short time, so what is left? Sweatshirts, workout pants, sweaters, and undergarments. When we get to our destination, I will have to go shopping for new clothes.

The oversized rolling red luggage bag barely closed when I finished packing it, and the closet still had so much left inside. But there is no more space, so sacrifices have to be made. The climbing gear, my favorite snowsuit, and skis are all replaceable, unlike our lives.

Although my stomach felt queasy, I fixed myself a peanut butter and jelly sandwich. A few hours had passed, and I needed to stick with the doctor's orders to eat.

The letter from Ethan stared at me from the kitchen counter, so I grabbed a drink and the envelope and headed for the couch. My head turned to the front door when a single thump, as though

115

someone's knuckles hit it once, drew my attention. No one was there when I peeked through the peephole, so I opened it to see if I had a delivery. A single long-stem red rose lay on the carpet with a tiny notecard attached that had one word written on it.

Never...

Chapter Fourteen-Run

When the glass dropped out of my hand, it shattered into a billion pieces on the floor. The letter in my hand crumpled in my grasp as I stared at a scarlet red rose and a single-word note that mocked me from the hall.

I looked down at the once smooth envelope that was now crushed in my grasp and knew that I wouldn't be reading it now.

My throat tightened, making breathing more difficult by the second, and my teeth rattled. Taking a deep breath, I cleared my mind and exhaled to collect myself enough to secure the door.

Ruger hopped from the couch when I ran to the door, slammed it shut, and locked it. He followed me to my room as I seized my rolling luggage and set it by the front door.

As I stared at its size, I realized traveling lighter would make more sense, so I ditched it and took a tote with two changes of clothes, my new wallet, and hygiene essentials.

I changed from my robe to all-black attire, pulled on black athletic sneakers, tucked my hair in a hat, and snatched a small bag of Ruger's food. A neighbor on the first floor would be my saving grace. We speed-walked down the hall, and I pushed the button repeatedly as if that would make it come faster.

When the elevator staggered open, it stunk like marijuana, so I covered my nose to keep from inhaling it.

Mrs. Jones is an older woman with tight white curls and a demanding stature whom Ruger loves to death. She babysits him for me on my long days at work, which I appreciate, but right now, her slow analytic gait to the door wore on my patience as I stood outside knocking. I pushed past her and pulled Ruger inside when she finally opened up.

"Ashley, is everything all right?" She asked.
"No. I need to leave. Can I please cut through and go out the back way?"
"Of course, dear. Do you want me to take Ruger for a bit?"
"That would be amazing. Ethan can pick him up later," I said.

I handed her his food, scratched him behind the ears, and kissed him goodbye. Leaving him is the hardest thing I have ever done, but I need to think about my little girl now. We are not safe.

Everything appeared quiet in the parking lot when I peered through the Venetian blinds. I slid the door open and made my way to the walking path gate that led to the recreational grounds next door.

The park walkway is attached to a massive soccer field with a baseball diamond on the far side that leads to a residential area. I strolled off the pavement and hopped the fence on the third base side.

 A dog barked in the yard a few houses away as I cut through the lawn of a two-story cottage-style yellow home with white trim. As I walked several blocks to the transportation center, the streetlights lit my way.

 When I arrived at the bus station, the man on the other side of the counter eyed me as I bought three tickets to leave for one person. A redhead stands out in a crowd, so I removed my hat and shook my hair.

 All the buses provided a restroom, so when I entered the first one, I went straight for it, switched clothes, stuffed my locks into a knit cap, and left the previous outfit in the bathroom.

 I turned my bag inside out to reveal a new exterior and took a seat in the back. After everyone boarded, I snuck out of the rear exit before the doors shut. I returned to the bathroom inside the station and altered my attire again. The reading glasses I put on blurred my eyes, but they helped with my disguise.

 I pulled on a snug pair of black pants, a long burgundy sweater, and a pair of old black knee-high boots. The driver on the second bus smiled at me as I boarded and handed her my ticket. I walked to the back of the bus much like before, sat in the back, and left again. This time I kept the same clothes and hopped on the next coach.

 A massive crowd of people piled into the third bus. The other two buses only held a sparse number of patrons, but this one was destined for New York City for the weekend.

Bodies blocked my escape as people stood around, trying to find a seat. Nausea made its way into my throat as my stomach quivered and my hands shook.

There were so many people touching me that I froze and sat down. But by the time the aisle emptied enough for me to leave, the driver closed the doors and got on his way. I thought running away would be easy, but I was mistaken.

A man came, slid next to me, and reeked of mint when he spoke. A flashback of my time in the cave hit me hard, and my hands gripped the cloth chair under me. I rocked forward and backward as my legs pressed together and anxiety clutched my chest. If I don't find another place to sit, I will lose it altogether and blow my cover.

"Let me out, please," I said to him.
"But we are going," he said.
"Please move. I can't stay in this seat."

He got out of my way, and I hid in the restroom. The dizziness from hyperventilating and the pounding in my chest made me almost faint, so I rested on the toilet with my head between my legs. I flinched when the door rattled against its frame and debated whether I should open it.

"Hello, is everything all right?" A woman's voice said.

When I opened the door, a woman with long, colored black hair and ashen skin grimaced at me. Her glimmering red shoes drew attention to her feet more than her blue and white checkered jumpsuit. She looked like a tall walking flag with ruby lipstick and blue eyeshadow.

"Listen, whatever you are going through will pass. Everything does. Getting all worked up about it in a bathroom on wheels will not help much. I have a spot near the restroom if you want to join me. That way, if you need to hide your feelings, you can do it without trampling a small child."
"I almost did that?"
"No, but it might have happened. Now, come on. Get off that dirty throne and come sit down," she said, wiggling her painted, manicured fingers at me.

I took the hand she offered me and the seat as well. We chatted for half an hour about her life, the city, and losing her husband.

"Here I am carrying on, and I didn't tell you my name. I'm Marilyn. Now, how about you? What's your story?" She asked.
"Not much to tell."
"I doubt that. How about when are you due?"
"How did you know?"

"You're glowing, darling. When pregnant, all women have a certain look on their faces. Rosy cheeks, illuminated complexion, and a habit of rubbing their belly," she smiled, nodding at my hand.

My hand touches it all the time now that I am aware. I thought about my interaction with Ethan at the hospital. Did I feel my abdomen when we talked? If so, did he know what it meant? He can't know. I can't imagine how he would look at me if he did. Having another man's baby would not go over well, especially when that man is a serial killer.
I stared out the window and said nothing. My weighted eyes couldn't remain open anymore, and I fell asleep.

The bus bounced over a pothole, jarring me awake as my head slapped against the glass. The woman beside me was gone, and so was my bag. I jumped out of my seat and searched all around. Red shoes appeared in front of me as I crawled under the seat, looking for my property.

"Honey, what are you doing?" She asked.
"Did you take my stuff?"
"Sit down. We have to talk," she said.
"About?"
"When you passed out, the sack slipped off your lap, and a wallet fell out. I'm not saying I was right,

but I peeked inside. Ashley, I know who you are and why you are running, and I would like to help," she said.

"How?"

"Well, I have a friend who has a condominium in Virginia Beach. This route runs right through it, drops a few people off, and then keeps going. Because it's in the colder months, she's in Florida. I just got off the phone with her, and she said it's free to use for a couple of months until you can find a place and settle in. Here's the code and the address."

"Why are you doing this for me?"

"Well, let's say our situations are similar, and I found myself in need. A stranger came to my aid and went out of her way for me as well. Never question God's gifts, sweetheart. If it weren't meant to happen, it wouldn't have," she said, patting my hand with hers.

I'm unsure if she means the baby is a gift or meeting her. Either way, I am thankful that I now have a destination to go to. The idea of being near a sandy beach bothered me to no end, but it was only temporary until I cashed my check and found a more permanent solution.

A road sign read that the beach was only fifty more miles away. If I can make it there, we can start over somewhere safe.

Chapter Fifteen-Bait and Switch

An idea came to Marilyn as we approached the last stop before reaching Virginia Beach. Our frame is similar, so switching clothes in the restroom would be easy.

The only problem I foresaw would be my hair, but Marilyn solved it with a box of temporary dye she keeps.

"Now, as soon as we stop, there won't be much time. I can do your makeup and wash mine off while the dye sets. The driver only gives us a twenty-minute break, so it may not be the best, but at least that beautiful head won't be red," she said.
"Marilyn, I appreciate everything you're doing for us," I said, taking her hand.
"It's not a problem," she said, squeezing my hand.

We made a mad dash to the bathroom as soon as the bus stopped. The shallow sink did little to shield our attire as she applied the dye like a pro. She scrubbed my head until it frothed and wrapped it in plastic wrap.
I cleaned up the edges around my face before she smudged makeup on me the way she did on herself. Looking like a flag is not my style, but I would do whatever it takes to keep us safe.
Our outfits fit each other's bodies perfectly. The age of our faces may give us away, but it's dark, and

people tend not to pay too much attention on these trips. They are too busy on their phones watching videos or reading a book.

Either way, we didn't intend on leaving anything up to chance, so I'm leaving now.

The money I have on me is enough to catch a ride and take city transit to my next location. Marilyn called from her phone for me, and I stayed in the bathroom.

No one would miss the zany lady who dressed like a spokesperson for the Fourth of July parade, but someone would look for me and my clothes.

The car showed up after about thirty minutes of waiting. As we drove away from the rest stop, I thought about what was next. I need to find an affordable place to stay, but I also want something nice.

The driver pulled into the city depot, and the bus I had abandoned at the last location sat unexpectedly at the curb.

"Shit," I said under my breath.
"Is there a problem, ma'am?" the woman said from the front seat.
"Yes. I need to go to the closest hotel to here instead."

She continued driving until we reached a dive motel which appeared to be the type of location they would house recently released prisoners. It's only for one night, so I sucked it up against my better judgment.

Once I entered my room, I removed the comforter, knowing it hadn't been washed in ages. The covers under the blanket appeared clean, so I laid down and rested my exhausted body.

The darkness disoriented me when I woke up, and I froze on my back with my fingers gripping the sheet. The shady motel room came into focus, and my heart rate normalized, but it took its time.

The moment I rolled out of bed and stood, vomit filled my mouth, so I held it there with my hand until I reached the bathroom. The greasy, cracked floor tile cut into my legs as I heaved crackers and water.

After washing my hands and brushing my teeth and hair, I left the musty restroom with no intention of returning.

Once I turned the lights on, I discovered that if I threw up on the carpet, it would just blend in. Its dirty, green, and red-stained status made my toes curl inside my shoes as I thought about how many bodily fluids covered the textured synthetic fiber.

"Gross," I said to the empty room.

The clock beside me read five, but the sun was cresting on the horizon, so I think the lazy hotel staff never changed it. I gathered the bag Marilyn gave me and put my hand on the doorknob but stopped before opening it.

My newfound paranoia has me checking and double-checking my surroundings more than I ever have in my entire life. As much as I didn't want to stand outside, anything was better than staying in this place for another second.

The front desk clerk let me use the phone to call for a lift to the station. They offered complimentary breakfast and cartons of milk, so I drank one of those and grabbed a bottle of water for the road.

The driver arrived promptly, and her cheerful voice perked me up as she greeted me with an enthusiastic smile.

"Good morning. Aren't we dressed festively this morning?" she said.

"Thanks. I need a ride to the bus station, please."

"Of course," she smiled.

She stayed silent throughout the trip, and I appreciated it. I'm still trying to wrap my head around what I am doing and what's next. I glanced over my shoulder often, and the girl upfront sensed my discomfort.

"Listen, no one is following us. I'm very observant when I drive, so if I see anything, I will tell you," she said, staring at me in the mirror.

"Thanks," I said, offering no explanation.

Once we arrived, I paid her a little extra for her discretion and climbed on a bus destined for the beach.

As we drove along, it bounced over every pothole the city offered, tossing my stomach into chaos as we made our way down the street. I looked around for the bathroom just in case but found out they didn't have one, so I sat nervously and hoped I wouldn't get sick.

The trip to the ocean strip took less time than I expected, and thankfully I didn't end up throwing up. Hotels lined the streets on either side, and the sidewalks bustled with tourists and locals, making me hesitate when getting off.

I'm a stranger in this place, and a part of me wanted to return to somewhere familiar. Starting over is never easy for me. It's not that I'm afraid. It's just such a hassle to meet people and learn the ins and outs of a new city.

My first order of business is to empty my bladder and find a clothing store to change into something else. The retail location I found carries a wide variety of style options but few of each item.

After using the restroom, I pulled size three jeans off the rack and headed into the changing room. When I tried to button them, about a half inch of extra belly prevented their closure. Nature works fast, and I am not prepared.

Blood volume is not the only thing increasing; so are my waistline and my appetite.

This type of pant is not practical, so I peeled them off, inside out, and left them on the ground. Before leaving the dressing room, I rubbed my belly in a circle and wondered if she could hear me.

The rack I grabbed the jeans from didn't have the next size, so I looked elsewhere and settled on stretchy knit leggings, an oversized sweatshirt, socks, and sneakers.

I removed all the tags, walked to the register, and paid for the outfit before leaving. The woman at the register told me that not a single time in her ten-year career has someone walked an entire outfit while wearing it to the checked-out counter.

She didn't bother to ask me where my other clothes were, and I am not one to volunteer information. My assumption is that old clothes are found in the dressing rooms often.

The flag top and bottom stayed behind for someone else who may wish to draw attention to themselves. Marilyn never mentioned wanting them back, so I assumed they were replaceable. Besides, I must blend in as I walk the boardwalk and peer out at the ocean.

Like my life, the waves rolled in and out to sea, washing the shore away and wearing it down. The crashing water shatters fragile shells, and yet people still pick them up and take them home, so I may still have a chance.

I daydreamed about escaping to a tropical island and raising my baby peacefully, but it's unrealistic, especially now that a killer is not the only one hunting us. I can't elude them all forever, but I prayed for our sake that if someone did find us, they would be coming to help, and not to hurt.

Chapter Sixteen-Scene of the Crime

Mills pulled her gun from its holster as soon as she spotted the rose in front of Ashley's threshold. Her soundless steps approached with caution as she worked her way to the open doorway.

Pieces of glass littered the ground, and dried orange juice stuck to the underside of her shoes. After sweeping every room, she kneeled and examined the chunky cup pieces more closely. There didn't appear to be any signs of blood, so that was a positive sign.

She called the crime scene team and let Ethan know that Ashley and Ruger have disappeared. A neighbor appeared in front of her with the flower from the carpet in her hand, startling Mills to her feet.

"Put that down. It's evidence."

The woman threw it away from her body, and it landed in the middle of the shattered pile. Mills rolled her eyes and ushered the neighbor out of the room.

"Did you hear anything last night or this morning?" Mills asked.

"Not a thing. Of course, I take a ton of medicine to help me sleep. Hell, a hurricane could plow through here and take me with it, and I wouldn't be the wiser," she giggled.

"Here's my card, and if you remember something, call me," Mills said, turning the woman back toward her place.

As soon as the neighbor's doors shut, the elevator opened, and Ethan moved briskly toward her with disheveled hair and wrinkled pajamas.

"Mills, what's happening? Where is Ashley?"
"I don't know," she said, trying to keep him from entering the room.

He tried pushing her aside, but she held him firm as he gawked at the fragmented glass and flower that decorated its center. His face transformed to that of someone in complete despair, as though he had just lost his best friend to a tragic accident.

"I don't understand. How did this happen with Ruger here? He would have let no one near her," he said, placing his hands on his head.
"Ethan, we don't know what happened yet, so don't get worked up."
"Ashley is missing, and you're telling me not to be upset? Mills, are you fucking kidding me? Where were the police getting donuts?"

Mills didn't have a chance to respond. Ruger ran straight towards them as Mrs. Jones waddled rapidly after him. He jumped right onto Ethan's chest and then hustled inside before they could stop him.

His excitement got the best of him as he lost his footing and glided through the sharp fragments on the floor, cutting himself. Blood droplets trailed throughout the space between the door and couch as he made his way to his favorite place on the furniture.

"Ruger, come here, dumbass," Ethan said, grabbing a towel.

The dog wiggled his nub and ran back to his master to treat the injuries he was oblivious of. Ethan wrapped the cloth around his lower back leg and squeezed it to stop the flow.

"Oh, dear. I'm sorry to bring him back so soon. I have a doctor's appointment that I forgot about. Please apologize to Ashley for me," Mrs. Jones said.
"Where is she?"
"I don't know, Ethan. Perhaps that sticky mess on the floor has something to do with it. Well, I must be going."

Mills passed Ethan the cornstarch from the cupboard to put on the dog's cut. Once the bleeding stopped, he hooked his leash around the bedroom doorknob and went inside.
The closet door stood open, and only a few items dangled from their hangers. The rolling luggage sat

half-filled underneath as though she had decided against it. He closed his eyes and tried to picture her favorite clothes—the ratty burgundy top.

"The sweater. Ashley would never part with it. It belonged to her mother, so she must have it with her," Ethan said.

"All right, that might be important. I plan on checking the local bus stops to see if she has left or is still in town."

"I can take my dog home and go too. Please let me help."

"Fine, stop touching things," Mills said, taking his hands off the counter.

After leaving Ashley's building, Mills called Ethan and told him to meet her at the bus station. When he arrived, she stood by her car with a plastic bag in her hand. The sack held wet, all-black clothing with red strands of hair stuck to it.

"I found these in a toilet tank in the restroom. I need to confirm that it is Ashley's."

He smoothed the crinkled sopping attire out on the hood of Mill's vehicle and verified it was, in fact, hers. She stuffed it inside the pouch and motioned for him to follow her. They stopped at a table full of sorted-out boxes labeled lost and found.

"The driver on a shorter round-trip route discovered some clothing in the bathroom. Ethan, go through these and let me know if any of them belong to Ashley."

Mills handed him a set of latex gloves and set an empty receptacle on the counter for sorting. He gingerly pulled them on his hands, picked up the fabric articles one at a time, and placed them inside the vacant box.

A t-shirt caught his eye, so he removed it and opened it to check out the front. It's his. He discarded it in her bedroom one night when he stayed over a couple of months ago and never asked for it back. Perhaps he wanted to have a reason to come back to her place if she left him in the future.

After several minutes of digging, he pulled out a pair of over-washed black jeans. The faded thighs, ripped knees, and frayed ankles had always been his favorite pair when she wore them with heels. He brought them to his nose and inhaled her scent deep into his lungs.

"Men are so gross," Mills said with a disgusting frown.

The security office waved at them from down the hallway. They brought up the surveillance footage from the last twenty-four hours and carried in an extra chair so they could comb through it together.

Ethan sat on Mill's right with his head resting on his palm and elbow on the table.

After several hours of watching, he spotted her buying tickets at the register. Her fiery red hair stood out as she shook it free from her hat. A killer may not have seen her sneaking in different outfits on and off the bus, but Ethan and Mills did.

She is trained, and he is familiar with her figure and her style, so it made finding out which one she took easy.

Of all places one could travel to, it had to be New York City. What a vast search area they will have to cover.

"What the heck is that lady wearing? She's dressed like a flag," Ethan said, pointing at the checkered outfit of the boarding woman.

"Ethan, people are just weird sometimes."

They returned to Ashley's place to find the door taped shut with crime scene tape and the apartment empty. Ethan asked Mills to let him stay and clean, so it wasn't a mess when she came home. Since he has a key to it, Mills doesn't give it a second thought and agreed.

She took a phone call in the hallway and stared at his calculated cleaning method as he finished sweeping the glass off the floor. Instead of grabbing a mop, which would be much faster, he diligently cleaned the sticky gunk off on his hands and knees with white vinegar.

"Ethan, my colleague, has informed me that the bus makes a pit stop in Virginia on its way to the city. It is possible that she got off there, so I am headed that way to review the cameras," she said.

"Why don't they send them?" He asked without looking up from the hardwood.

"I like to take the same route, view the landscaping, and the rest stops on the way. It helps me climb into the mind of the person I am looking for. Why don't you come along?"

This got his attention. Going after her would show her how much she meant to him and that he would do anything to find her. He stood up and put away his supplies.

"I would love to, but I have to drop Ruger off at the kennel first."

They stopped at his apartment before getting on the road, and Mills waited in the car for him. His place is close to Ashley's, so they arrived in no time. When he exited the building, Mills swore under her breath.

Wrapped around Ethan's throat like a scarf on a chilly day sat his camera.

"Nope. Take it back inside," she demanded.

"But what if we need to photograph something for evidence? The quality would be better than your cell phone," he said, pleading his case.

"After what Ashley said at the hospital about caring more about that freaking thing, are you going to show up with it around your neck?"

Ethan sighed, and his shoulders dropped. Without a word, he exited the car, ran into the house, and returned a minute later, minus the camera.

The flicking of his nail on his tooth and intermittent aggressive leg rubbing plucked Mill's last nerve. She tried to understand his extreme fidgeting, but the overwhelming urge to shoot him made her pull over.

"Stop it, Ethan. For the love of God, you're annoying."

"I'm sorry. I'm just used to having my camera to keep my hands and mind busy."

She shook her head and kept driving until a gas station appeared on the side of the highway. Determined to solve her problem and his, Mills went inside and searched for something to pacify him.

The cashier rotated something in his hand when she went to the counter. He flicked it in a circle flat on his hand, then turned it on its side between two fingers and spun it again.

"Are those for sale?" She asked.

"No," he said, too busy watching it to acknowledge her.

"Look, I can give you ten dollars right now for it," Mills offered.

"Twenty?"

"Deal," Mills said, passing him the money, desperate for peace.

The minute she handed Ethan the fidget toy, all his cares went out the window, and she continued driving without blowing his brains out.

Chapter Seventeen-Safe

After walking the boardwalk for over an hour, I gathered enough courage to remove my shoes and try to walk on the sand.

I longed to place my feet in the ocean again and let the waves wash over my tired body. Yet fear grips me with the first shift of the sand between my toes, and I recoil.

Tears poured down my disappointed face as I gazed at all the people on the beach without a care in the world, loving the grittiness of it as I once did.

I quickly replaced my shoe and returned to solid ground. I may try another day when I have more time and fewer things to worry about.

The walkway is quiet as I move forward, looking for the answers I seek. Is this the best thing I can do for us? Run away with no place to go. Sure, I have a condo for now, but then what? Dwelling on the unknown was getting me nowhere, so I headed to the place Marilyn's friend kindly offered.

The luxury high-rise sits across from the beach, and almost every floor has a balcony. Outside, a pool with a bar beside it supplied refreshments for the owners who lived in the building and a magnificent entertaining space.

When I stepped through the door, it transported me into the world of the rich and famous; on my left, two restaurants, and on my right, a total gym and massage facility. The concierge at the desk waved at me with a gratuitous smile.

"I can help you here," she said.

"My friend said to give you this when I came in," I said, offering her the note with the keypad and address information.

"Yes, Marilyn, we have been expecting you. This way."

Marilyn? I didn't correct her as she walked to the elevators and climbed on with me. The transparent elevator glass gave me a breathtaking view of the ocean and surrounding area as we made our ascent. My tour guide explained the ins and outs of the building, what it offers, and security measures.

When she opened the door to where I would stay for the next few months, free of charge, I almost passed out.

It was more than just a condominium. It was a two-level, two-bedroom flat with a wrap-around balcony.

"If you need anything further, call me at the front desk. The number is on the fridge," the concierge said, walking away.

I don't know who Marilyn's friend is, but she is loaded. The marble floors and furniture are top-of-the-line. She left nothing to chance. A large beach tote sat on the counter in the kitchen with a note, and I walked over to read it.

Ashley,

I know things are hard right now, but you have been at rock bottom, and there is nowhere to go but up from here. I hope the items inside provide you with some comfort during this trying time.

Your new friend,

Joyce
P.S. Marilyn says hello.

The bag held a book of vouchers for the restaurant, coupons for free massages, a gift card to a local clothing store, and a plush white robe.

I grabbed a seat next to the countertop, put my face in the crook of my arm, and cried. What a wonderful gift she has left to help ease my pain.

How lucky am I to have met such an amazing woman? Fate has dealt me an ugly blow but has returned with kindness. I peered down at my hand, rubbed my stomach, and looked at the refrigerator—time to feed the little one and me.

The fridge came stocked with enough food to host a small army.

There is milk, juice, fruit, vegetables, healthy snacks, and a loaf of bread. Inside the freezer, frozen strawberry non-fat yogurt with real berries, a bag of mixed antioxidant frozen fruit, and plenty of frozen vegetables. I rifled through the cupboards and found a blender to make a healthy smoothie.

A small desk by the window supplied a pen and notepad so I could start my to-do list. I need to do everything in one go to have minimal outside exposure. As I put pen to paper, I became stumped after writing the first line.

Buy clothes!

That's it. That is all there is to do. I have everything I could ever want here except a closet with things to wear. The only thing left beyond that is finding a more permanent place to stay, but that doesn't have to be done now.

I polished off my drink, pulled my hair into a ponytail, and headed shopping for clothes. The credit for my new wardrobe is for a boutique on the main street. They carry a variety of dresses, leggings, tunics, sweaters, sandals, and matching accessories.

The shop owner is about my age and half a head taller, with bleach-blonde curls and tan skin. She treated me as though I were a sister to her and spun me around in each outfit. I loved everything about it. I've never dealt with a saleswoman with so much attention to detail.

Perhaps it is her job to fill my bag with all these essentials, but it takes a special kind of person to make you feel as though they have known you their whole life.

Although the prices are high, you get what you pay for. I left with three new outfits that covered all the bases from head to toe, including hats.

A t-shirt in a shop window found across the street pulled me inside. Its statement couldn't have been more straightforward or meant for me as I stared at it on the mannequin.

You are worth fighting for…

I grabbed the grey version with pink letters from the table, found a pair of jean jeggings to go with it, and a white pair of tennis shoes. The man at the register smiled widely when I set my things down.

He didn't speak at first. He just stared to the point where my stomach became uneasy. His eyes wandered up and down me, and my fingers coiled into my palms. I needed to leave as a meltdown was coming.

As soon as the change hit the counter, I grabbed it and left the store immediately. A voice hollered after me as my pace quickened, and I began to run.

He's coming. I thought as I continued to evade him.

A woman stopped my advancement and held my shoulders. I shook so hard, and my heart thumped so fast that I came dangerously close to passing out.

"He's just trying to give you your things," she said, reaching around my distraught frame.

When she returned her hands, all my shopping bags were in them. I abandoned the store in such a hurry that I left everything behind. My legs buckled, and I went down to the rough ground in a heap of despair. What am I doing?

"Do you want me to call someone for you?" The woman asked.
"No. I need a minute to collect myself, is all," I said, wiping the snot from my nose.
"Well, why don't you do it from the bench next to you instead of on the concrete," she said, handing me a tissue.
"Thank you."
"No, problem. This is my place, so if you need anything, I'm only a few feet away," she offered as she made her way back inside.

Everything is happening so fast, and I may have overplayed my ability to do this on my own. I should have let Ethan in and let him help me through it, but I have doubts about our continued relationship.
Staying with him now would be for the wrong reasons and would be selfish. He's not obligated to stay with us because of what happened while we were together. Besides, he would never accept my

baby as his own, and I would not allow him to treat her differently.

Sure, it would be nice for her to have a father figure, but what kind of life would it be for her?

Would it be like mine and be second in line for affection after his camera? Or would she be in third place and nothing more than a participation ribbon for him?

We deserve to be happy after what happened, and I will not let a killer, the FBI, or Ethan take that away from us.

Chapter Eighteen-Not Ashley

Mills and Ethan arrived at the station in New York City after several daunting hours of congested roadways and torrential storms. The terminal bustled with heavy foot traffic leaving and arriving for business and pleasure purposes.

Most of these people are tourists looking for the adventure of a big city but don't realize how dangerous it can be.

The bus driver viewed the photo of Ashley over his glasses and then gave it back to Ethan.

"Nope, I haven't seen her. I would have remembered that hair."

"This image is not as clear, but it is from a bus station in Virginia Beach," Mills said.

"Yes, I remember her now. Her hat covered her head, so perhaps I didn't see it. She kept coughing and had a disposable mask on her face. Her sweater was old and torn, like it had been worn thousands of times. It must be her favorite," he smiled, handing the photograph back.

"Thanks," Mills said.

They walked inside the building to view the security footage from when the bus arrived. It showed she got into a yellow cab, so Mills contacted the company to get the driver's route.

Ashley's taxi dropped her off in Soho, a square mile of shopping, bars, restaurants, bakeries, and museums.

The only thing he remembered was that she was quiet and didn't say a word to him even as she climbed out in front of a famous coffee establishment.

They drove to the shop, sat by the window, and questioned the employees. Ashley didn't stay, she took her beverage to go, but they had no intention of giving up.

Searching such a vast radius together would be a waste of time and almost impossible. Mills telephoned the first precinct to send out a BOLO for the patrolling officers to aid in the search.

Mills sent the image of Ashley from the depot and the one Ethan provided, then they spilt up. Two heads are better than one, and they can cover more ground twice as fast, with the police making up the difference.

Ethan and Mills showed Ashley's picture to every street vendor and performer along their routes. After an hour of looking, Ethan grew frustrated with the lack of cooperation from the locals. They either didn't care enough to help or flat-out refused altogether. A streak of burgundy caught his attention, entering an alley up ahead.

He bumped passed several sidewalk patrons and rounded the corner to find a homeless man digging through the trash. On his back, he wore Ashley's mother's sweater. Ethan seized the old man and forced him into the brick wall behind him.

"Where is she?" Ethan hollered in his face.
"Who?"
"The woman whose top this belongs to. Where?"
"I don't know. The lady came out of a store down the street and handed it to me. It's cozy," He smiled, rubbing the sleeves of it.
"Take it off, now," Ethan ordered.
"No, it's mine now. She said I could have it."
"Take it off, or I will," Ethan seared.
"Fine. Don't get so angry, son."
"I am not your son," he yelled, snatching the knit fabric away. "Take me to the place where this exchange occurred now."

They walked several blocks to a high-end boutique that sold pantsuits, professional attire, and accessories to match. He called Mills upon arrival when the business owner refused to give him any information about their clientele. The owner's face and reluctance to speak changed with one flash of Mill's FBI credentials.

"Yes, she came in about a half hour ago and bought an all-white pantsuit and matching hat, Though I don't remember her hair being red. Then again, she changed her entire outfit in the dressing room and paid while wearing them. A tad odd, if you ask me," she said in a judgmental tone.

"Thanks," Mills said.

After contacting the station with an updated description, they stayed together, got in the car, and drove around. Spotting someone dressed entirely in uncolored attire makes searching easier.

Vagrants, shoppers, and people on their lunch breaks cluttered up the sidewalks and crosswalks as they made their way down every street. Mills sighed as she checked her mirror for a third time.

"We are being followed."

"What? Who is it?" Ethan asked, looking behind them.

"I don't know. Hang on," she said, taking the corner too fast.

Mills took several right-hand turns to be sure she wasn't being paranoid, but at every corner, the car reappeared. She gunned the engine on a straightaway and blew through a red light, but that didn't stop their stalker. Ethan clenched the handle above him tightly as Mills drove recklessly down the road. Her white knuckles spun the wheel on a residential street, where she slammed on her brakes and blocked the car behind them.

"What are you going to do?"

"Ethan, stay in the car."

The driver reversed the car, tried to elude but miscalculated the wheel, and drove into the back end of a van.

Mills pulled her gun out and ordered the person out of the driver's seat. As soon as he exited, she recognized him as a reporter hanging around Ashley's apartment building for the last several days.

"What the hell are you doing?" Mills said, holstering her weapon.

"Chasing the story. Ashley ran, didn't she? I knew it. The killer is coming after her, and she is running from him. I am so going to get a promotion for this."

"Get back in the car and wait for the police. By following us, you could put not only yourself in danger but Ashley as well. The story is not worth your life."

Ethan stood outside the car, watching the interaction between the reporter and Mills. The weasel is using Ashley to advance his career, and he doesn't like it. He was prying into her private life and stalking her while taking pictures. He stormed at the journalist, but Mills stepped in the middle.

"Ethan, I know you're upset, but pummeling him for doing his job will not help."

"Get his camera. I want to see what he has on there," he said as he burned through the man's face with his eyes.

"I have nothing to hide, and none are inappropriate," the man said, handing Mills the camera.

Ethan hovered over her shoulder as she scrolled through them. The pictures documented everyone, and everything connected to the investigation. He even had an image of the crime scene tape sealing off Ashley's apartment door. Ethan snatched the camera from Mills, thrust it into the reporter's chest, and returned to the agent's ride.

Once Mills finished giving her statement to the local police, she crossed the road and headed back to the car. The officer taking the reporter's information called her back. A person matching Ashley's description was spotted a few short blocks away. Mills gunned the car and drove quickly to the location she was last seen.

Ethan, desperate to see Ashley again, jumped out of the vehicle before it stopped and spun the person dressed in white around.

"What the fuck?" Ethan whispered under his breath.

It is not Ashley. The woman's eyes gave her away despite the mask she wore. Mills ordered her to remove it and the hat so they may question her.

After several minutes, the only thing they pulled from the woman was her name, Marilyn. She found the outfit on the bus, and no one claimed it, so she did.

"Liar," Ethan blurted, advancing toward her.
"Ethan, enough," Mills said, moving him back. "Marilyn, here is my card. If anything else comes to mind, please call."
"Mills, she knows more than she is saying. Ashley would never give up her mother's sweater. Something more had to have happened."
"It doesn't matter. Thanks to her, we know Ashley changed her clothes again, and we missed it somewhere along the line. So, we need to go back and retrace our steps."

Ethan watched the woman standing in front of a storefront, waiting for a cab. He knew in his heart that she knew more than what she was letting on, but perhaps Mills was right. What if they missed something?

They have Marilyn's hotel address and room number so they can return to her later if they discover she lied. But for now, they head back to the bus station to speak with the driver again.

Chapter Nineteen-Lonely

Sleeping in a stranger's bed is difficult, but hearing the ocean outside calling to me and not being able to go to it, makes falling asleep a challenge.

I don't think I have ever felt so lonely in life. At least when Ethan didn't stay the night, Ruger kept me company. Now it's just me, lying here alone, wishing I wasn't.

The plush mattress and luxury blankets should make it easier for me to transition into dreamland, but the problem is whenever I hear a noise, my eyes flicker open, and I wonder if he's found me. Is the creaking coming from the other room his careful footsteps? Or just my mind playing tricks on me again, like before?

Up and down all night long, I barely slept at all. As I lie here and stare out the balcony window, watching the waves crash ashore, I think about Ethan. If he were here, his arms would wrap around me, and we'd love this view together. Tears burst out of me regardless of how little I wanted to cry, along with watery secretions from my nose.

"Snap out of it, Ashley."

The covers flew off me and slid onto the floor in a pile as I forced myself out of bed. I grabbed the robe given to me and called the concierge to make me a massage appointment. It's free, so why not enjoy it?

The spa needed me downstairs in about one hour, leaving me with time to take a hot shower, eat a piece of toast, and sit outside and enjoy the view. The water is now abandoned, but a few people milled about collecting shells or taking their morning run on the sand. That used to be me, enjoying the unevenness of its textured grit as it helped sculpt my leg muscles and build up stamina.

After stuffing the last bite of browned bread into my mouth, I brushed my teeth and headed to the lobby.

The spa's tasteful, warm, welcoming color palette and cheerful staff put me at ease as the masseuse handed me a towel to ready myself. I climbed my almost naked frame onto the table and closed my eyes. The woman's palms on my back magically worked at pressing the kinks and knots out of my stiff spine.

She stopped to gather more oil, and when her hands returned, I froze in fear. The way she touched my thighs and stroked my greasy flesh came too close in similarity to what the mountain man did when he rubbed me. My entire frame and muscles stiffened to stone.

Salty water dribbled out of my eyes as a flashback struck me like a car, and I came crashing down to the floor. The masseuse came to me with her arms in surrender, trying to relax me, but I couldn't look at her. I snatched my robe from the black cubby holding her supplies, stuffed myself into it, and ran out of the room.

The elevator button came close to being damaged from bashing it so many times. The spa employee and concierge stared at me in pity and disbelief as the doors to the elevator clanked closed. My limbs failed me, and I went to the carpet for comfort.

The cab stopped on the floor before mine, and another passenger joined me.

"Are you okay?" A man's voice said as he placed a hand on my shoulder.

"Don't touch. Don't touch, Doooooon't," I screamed at him.

"I'm sorry," he said, shying away.

When the ride ended, I sprinted to my living quarters, slammed the door, and frantically locked the door behind me. My feet moved like lightning as I traveled to the bath, turned the water on hot, and scrubbed my filthy, slippery skin raw. I remained there, sitting on the harsh white surface, bawling until the water ran cold and forced me to retreat.

My body curled its bare self into a fetal ball, much like the baby inside me, and fell asleep under the warm covers on my king-size mattress.

The nightmare became so real that I thought the killer might lie next to me. I couldn't move my arms or head, and something leaked between my stiff legs. He found me and hurt me again. Afraid to stir or speak, I remained stuck until the telephone on the table by the bed forced my brain to react. When I turned my head toward the jingle, the space next to me was empty. I'm not being held prisoner, as I thought.

I mustered up the courage and strength to snatch the annoying phone from the receiver.

It was the front desk calling to check on me, but I hung up as another bit of liquid dripped and drained onto my inner thigh. I reached down, and terror overcame me when I brought it up as blood discolored my fingers.

I threw the blanket off, and a small, smudged stain at different drying stages spotted the sheets beneath me. The room around me shrank to the size of a closet as I shuffled to the bathroom. What does this mean? Am I losing her? Did all my paranoid antics take God's gift to me away?

The wadded-up ball of toilet paper in my underwear scratched my tender flesh as I finished dressing and called for a ride to the hospital. My lower limbs moved like a sloth as I approached the triage nurse at the emergency room.

"What can I do for you today?" The woman asked without looking at me.

"I...I think..., I don't know...I..."

I'm stumped. If I say it, will it make it true? I thought about turning around and leaving, but I needed answers. The nurse came from behind the transparent partition and placed her hand on my arm.

"You are safe here. Whatever it is, we can help you."
"I think I am losing my baby," I said as tears spilled over my lids.
"Oh, dear. Come with me," she said, taking me by the elbow.

She ushered me into a room, brought me a gown, and handed me a warm blanket.

"An ultrasound tech is coming down now, and the doctor will be in after," she said, leaving the room.

I switched to the paper outfit she supplied and sat in the chair instead of getting on the bed. Within minutes a young girl with dark brown hair, green eyes, and pale skin rolled a machine into the room. Her oversized navy-blue scrubs did nothing to hide her slight frame as she set up her equipment.
She turned to me with a soft smile and padded the mattress with her palm.

"It's time."
"I'm scared," I said, not moving.
"Most of the time, these things are normal responses to your body changing."
"Most of the time?"

"Come on. Let's get started," she said, reaching out to me.

She squirted warmed liquid onto my lower abdomen and moved the probe around, looking for signs of life. The more she searched, the more nervous I became.

"Ashley, how far along are you?" she asked.
"A couple of weeks."
"Well, that explains a lot. I need to do an internal to find anything," she said as she removed the tool from my belly.
"Is that the only way?"
"No. To be sure, you will also need to have two blood tests taken about two days apart."

She snatched the wand, slipped a condom over it, and helped me place my legs in the stirrups. I have allowed nothing inside me since the physician did the exam after my rescue from the mountain. I don't know why I expected time to have made a difference, for as soon as the shaft of the tool entered, I screamed.

"I'm so sorry. Did I hurt you?" The technician asked, removing the transducer.
"Please, I want to leave now."
"Wait and meet with the doctor, please. I know you're scared, but it is important to be checked."

I nodded my head in understanding and stayed until the doctor came in. She is an older woman, around sixty, with white hair pulled into a ponytail and supple lips.

"Ashley, I'm Dr. Kerin. The nurse told me you have some spotting. When did this start?"

"This morning," I said, sniffling.

"And the ultrasound is too uncomfortable for you to finish?"

Instead of responding with words, I avoided eye contact and stared at the tile.

"I recommend you have blood drawn today, and then in two days, please come back and have it drawn again. We measure what's called your hCG levels. These are the indicators of the development of the embryo. Once I receive your lab results, I will contact you and let you know. In the meantime, I want you to take it easy for the next few days."

"Okay," I said with a nervous smile.

She left the room, and the technician turned the television in the room on for me while I waited. The news came on with a breaking story just as the phlebotomist entered for the blood draw. She prepped the vein and inserted the needle as I listened.

'A woman found murdered this morning in New York City could have a link to an elusive killer. A source inside the police department confirmed a connection to the Cavern Killer even though initial statements of denial came from the FBI. The woman, traveling from North Carolina to the city on a tourist bus, endured a brutal beating and appeared to have suffered significant torture before her untimely death. Police will not further comment on the matter as it is an ongoing investigation. The family of Marilyn Springfield released a statement early this morning, and we will keep you apprised of any further developments as they come in....'

A photo of Marilyn came across the screen and disappeared. My heart broke into a million pieces and crashed to the floor in seconds. *Tortured.* She wore my clothes, and he followed them. Now she's dead, and it's my fault.

I grabbed my things, dressed, and left without proper discharge.

He's coming for me. Perhaps, not right this minute, but he's on his way. It takes several codes to enter the public building, but I don't feel safe anymore. I need to move again before it's too late.

Chapter Twenty-Let Him In

After contacting several furnished apartment buildings, I received a call back from one that interested me. We needed somewhere safe but close to the hospital, so I could still have my bloodwork done.

The respondent, a lady named Deb, agreed to meet me at the apartment. He's coming for us, and I need to keep moving, so he doesn't catch up.

When my driver pulled up to the building, I knew this would be the one. It is only a few short blocks from the boardwalk and a few miles from the medical center.

The living quarters came furnished and stocked with everything you would need except for food and the clothes on my back. I stepped onto the balcony and inhaled the ocean breeze as it drifted over my face. One couldn't ask for a better view of the body of water before me than this.

"I'll take it."

We signed a lease agreement saying I wouldn't destroy the place, and she handed over the keys. To enter the building, the stairwell upstairs, and my apartment, you must have a code, and all three codes are different. The level of security made my decision to stay that much easier. Unless the killer is Spiderman, he won't be able to reach us.

After taking down all the information I needed to enter, I left to gather my things from the condominium. My only regret is not being able to use all the restaurant vouchers, but I would rather be hungry and safe than full and in danger.

After I unloaded my clothes in the new apartment, I walked down to the boardwalk. The beach is full of vacationers and people stopping to see the ocean on their way home from work. I want to walk in the water, but going in requires touching the sand. If someone carried me and placed me in a lounge chair, I could at least let the salty liquid wash over me.

I miss Ethan. He and I could talk about anything without fear of it going further than the two of us. I trust him, but I don't want to see him hurt, not by the killer or me.

A couple carrying a baby approached me and asked to take their picture. The husband and wife are new parents enjoying their first ocean trip with their newborn. Too bad the baby is too young to remember, but that is what the photo is for.

After taking several shots from different angles, I returned their camera to them and continued down the walkway. A cellular store came up on my left, and I thought about it. If I buy a disposable phone and keep the conversation brief, it can't be tracked as easily. This way, Ethan and the FBI will know I am safe without giving away my location.

Using scissors provided by the employee, I tore open the package, activated it, and added minutes. I started dialing Ethan's number, then hesitated.

My thumb hovered over the image of the green circle with the white handset in the middle. If he came, then what?

The only thing I offer is my presence and conversation. Would that be enough for him? What would be the benefit to have him around? Sure, it would be nice not to be alone, but at what cost? I closed the phone and thought about it some more. Freshly grilled food wafted through my sinuses, drawing me to a nearby restaurant. They have outdoor seating, which is nice, but I prefer to sit inside out of the sun. A young man came and set a menu in front of me with a promise to return.

I sifted through the choices and contemplated on what I thought was my final decision until a juice burger sizzled its way past me, changing my mind. I stalked the man's plate from two tables away as he placed a too-hot fry in his mouth, scorching it.

That's what I want. Nothing is better than a gourmet burger with cheddar cheese, bacon, lettuce, tomato, and fries. But then I remembered I couldn't have bacon or potatoes, so I ordered the burger with no bacon and macaroni and cheese instead.

My meal came fresh from the kitchen, with steam billowing above the cheesy pasta. Choosing not to get second-degree burns on the roof of my mouth as the other patron did, I waited for it to cool.

When I took the first bite, the burger melted in my mouth, and I moaned in satisfaction. With every chomp of my jaw, the back of the burger slid further off the toasted bun and fell apart. My fingers picked at the remnants of it until all signs of its existence disappeared.

The macaroni cooled enough for me to try it. The smooth melty cheese stuck to my fork, leaving a string of it connecting us. I rotated it around the prongs and took another bite, but my belly soon ran out of space, so I took the leftovers home.

When I entered the empty apartment and peered around the space, an overwhelming loneliness overshadowed my mood. I wanted someone to talk to about this amazing burger place I just ate at, but there was no one there, not even Ruger.

I took the disposable out of my pocket, dialed Ethan's number, and without hesitation, hit call. He didn't answer. I imagine he didn't want to pick up a random call from some stranger, so he ignored it.

The phone rang in my hand, making me drop it. I picked it up, and Ethan's number appeared on the screen.

"Hello?"
"Ashley?" Ethan's voice said, sounding hopeful.
"Yes, it's me, but…."
"Where are you? We are worried sick," he said.
"I can't tell you. Not yet".

"Please, tell me where you are, and I will come to you. I am not mad, and I promise I will keep you safe," he pleaded.

"It's not that simple. There are some stipulations."

"Anything. Whatever it takes. Just tell me," he said.

"You can't touch me or ask questions. I'm afraid that you won't be happy with me if you do. Not only that, but I am also worried that the man who is after me will hurt you, and I would never forgive myself if that happened," I explained.

"Mills will be there. She won't let anything happen. We need to know where you are, though."

"Is she listening?"

"No. She isn't here."

"Good. I don't want anyone but you to come, so please, don't involve her?"

"Deal. What is the address?" He asked.

"When you arrive, I will have to let you in. Security is tight."

"No problem. Now, where are you?"

After giving him my location, I sat on the couch and waited. In about seven hours, Ethan will be here.

I chewed my nails down to the cuticle and made one bleed, so I shuffled into the bathroom to check the medicine cabinet. The Band-Aid box left by the earlier tenant sat empty on the glass shelf, so I started a list of things to shop for in the morning.

Besides food, I needed hair and body products, water, and Band-Aids.

The elbow I'm using to hold me up slides forward as I doze off while writing. My last words looked like a child writing with a crayon. The tropical sun and full stomach made me tired early, so I grabbed the blue comforter from the bed and curled up on the faux leather couch.

The volume on the phone, now too low, barely rang above a whisper at three-thirty in the morning.

"Hello?"
"Ashley, I'm outside."
"Coming," I said while yawning.

The sparsely lit stairwell to the bottom floor slowed my descent. As fluorescent lights flickered above me, I held the railing on the way down, and dirt and fuzzy debris shifted as I passed. The overwhelming urge to grab a broom and sweep overcame me, but I'll save that for another day.

Ethan's awkward wave at me through the external door made me smile. No matter what happened or how I may have felt, I was thrilled to see him.

As soon as he cleared the door, he physically tried to engage with me.

"Remember the rules," I said, stepping away.
"This is hard," he said, taking a step back.
"I know, but this is the only way for now."
"I understand."

He followed me up the three flights of stairs with his eyes on my backside the whole time. I can sense when someone is looking at me inappropriately, but I can't blame him, for we haven't been intimate in weeks.

While typing the code into my apartment, Ethan eyed me with intense anticipation, making me nervous. I hope he can control his urge to put his hands on me, or I will have to ask him to leave. Once inside, he placed his bag on the unmade bed and followed me.

We walk down the hallway together as I give him a quick tour of the apartment. The bathroom is on the right next to the laundry area, and the main living space supplied a desk on the right-hand side with a dinette close by. On the opposite wall, the cozy living room is across from an efficient kitchen.

His trigger finger fluttered as he examined all the natural woodwork of the building. He wanted to photograph it.

"Get your camera. I know you have it somewhere," I said, rolling my eyes.
"No, I left it at home," he said with a grin.
"Really? I'm glad but also sad because this place is amazing."
"Ashley, I'm sorry."
"For what?"

"Everything I have done and everything I will do in the future. I will do anything to make you happy. You are all that matters to me, and I love you."

"Ethan, I'm so tired. Can we pick this up tomorrow?"

"Of course," he said, motioning for me to go first.

Though he slept on one side of the bed, being here comforted me even if he couldn't touch me. The loneliness inside me floated away as I fell into a deep and peaceful sleep.

Chapter Twenty-One - The Story

Ethan's hand rested heavily on my waist as my belly tightened, and my hyperventilating woke him.

He removed his hand, jumped up, and moved in front of me. Tears soaked my pillow as they cascaded down the right side of my face like an endless waterfall.

"I didn't mean to upset you," he sighed while combing his fingers through his hair. "What can I do?"
"Leave."
"What? Ashley, I'm not going anywhere. Please, tell me how to help."

There is nothing he can do for me. I'm frozen on this mattress until my mind and body decide I am no longer in danger. Excessive moisture surged into my mouth as morning sickness reared its ugly head and forced me to act. I sprinted to the bathroom, locking the door behind me so Ethan couldn't come in. The painful retching lasted several minutes and painted the bowl with undigested dinner from the night before.
The door rattled as Ethan begged to come in from the other side.

"Do not come in here."
"Are you sick?"

"Yes. It may have been the burger I ate last night." I said as I leaned against the pale green wall next to the toilet.

I didn't lie. The burger may have caused me to throw up, but the more likely culprit is the baby growing inside my uterus. At least now I have an explanation for going to the hospital for the needed lab work.

After brushing my teeth and washing my palms, I opened the door. Ethan stood with his hands on his hips like a disappointed parent about to scold their child.

"What if you have food poisoning?"
"I will go get checked out."
"I'm coming with you," he said, grabbing his shoes.
"No. I am not a baby that needs coddling. Stay here."

He made a noise under his breath as I walked away, but I didn't care. I hustled down the stairs and out the door to my waiting ride. The same nurse recognized me at the triage desk when I entered the hospital and took me back to a room.

"The lab will be here in a bit," the nurse said before leaving.

A bit turned into nearly an hour, and I thought about walking out, but I needed to have this bloodwork done. The phlebotomist who came through the curtain apologized for the wait as she prepped my vein. Her furrowed brow and constant sighing led me to believe her day was going wrong. I reached into my purse, took out the massage vouchers I could never use, and handed them to her.

She covered her mouth to stifle her crying, then hugged me before I could stop her. I pulled myself away from her uncomfortable embrace and headed to the lobby.

That is where I found Ethan talking to a little boy with an oversized bandage on his knee, and I grimaced. Someday he will make a wonderful father, but I doubt he will ever want that with me now that I am tainted.

I kept going right out the door. As soon as my hand opened the cab door, Ethan intercepted me.

"Ashley, wait."
"Ethan, did you follow me here?"
"What is the big deal if I sat in the waiting area?"
"I asked you to wait at my place. Why didn't you listen?"
"Ashley, I am not Ruger. You can't order me to stay," he huffed as I continued walking.

His pace quickened as he worked to keep up with my quick steps. There was nothing more to say about it, and I didn't want to talk anymore, but he was not going anywhere, so I turned into a diner.

The least he could do was buy me breakfast since he insisted on stalking me.

I took a seat by a giant window with a view of the pier and ignored him while I reviewed the menu. The waitress came, took our orders, and brought each a glass of water with lemon.

Ethan intertwined his fingers and placed his elbows on the table across from me.

"What did the hospital say?"
"Ethan, no questions, remember?"
"Do you want to go swimming later?"
"Ethan, I can't step on the sand," I snapped, annoyed at another question.
"How about I carry you?"
"How are you supposed to carry me without touching me?" I said in a sarcastic tone.
"After breakfast, can we at least give it a shot?"
"Sure."

We ate in silence when the food arrived, and his eyes followed my hands with every bite of my waffle. His sharp facial features carried a shadow from going days without shaving. I missed caressing his smooth cheeks right after he swiped a razor across them. Ethan saw me gazing, and I turned my head, not wanting him to sense my longing.

When he parted his lips to speak, our waitress returned with the check, interrupting his chance. We walked down a few storefronts, where Ethan paid for a lounger for me and a regular chair for himself.

He pressed the chairs deep into the earth while I waited on solid ground. He peeled off his top, revealing his tan, ribbed abdomen, and something inside me stirred.

My breath caught in my throat as he returned, stood before me, and waited. My fingers wanted to feel his body all over. Perhaps that was the key. If I feel him, but he keeps his hands off, it may not be triggering. My pointer brushed it over his washboard stomach. He smiled at my effort, but I knew it might not help us get me in the water.

"Ashley, close your eyes."
"Why?"
"Do you trust me?"
"Of course," I said, shutting my lids.
"I'm going to tell you a story, and I want you to not only listen to it, but I also want you to put the imagery inside your head. It would be best if you focused for this to work," he insisted.

I nodded my understanding and kept my eyes closed.

"There once was a beautiful red-haired maiden whom people across the land adored. But she is afraid of heights, and her home is on a cliff, so she could never leave. Food and supplies had to be taken across the rickety rope bridge to her daily. Every day, whoever made the deliveries tried to help her across. The townspeople felt sorry for her. She missed all the festivals, every event, and any opportunity to be social because of her terrible fear. One day, a woman with the stature and strength of a man arrived in town with a solution. She crossed the vast walkway, scooped up the cliff-bound lady, and had her shut her eyes as she carried her across the shaky ground to the other side. When she released the maiden's body on the other side, she asked her to open her eyes to see her new surroundings. Open your eyes, Ashley."

The ocean water washed over my feet as the waves crashed into the shore. He did it. My brain became so focused on the story and the reality that I couldn't focus on him being a man or touching me. I twisted my frame to see him and became wild with excitement.

"Ethan, you did it."
"Honestly, I didn't think it would work," he said as he sat beside me.
"Well, I am happy it did," I said, reaching over and placing my hand on his.

Ethan made more progress with me today than I have in the last several days on my own.
We lounged in front of the water until the sun's intense rays became unbearable. I got up without thinking and froze in place when the gritty particles beneath me filled in between my toes.

Ethan snatched and hauled me across the terrain, weaving through people like an obstacle course. His rapid, uneven steps gained ground in seconds, giving my head little time to react to his touch. My legs shook violently as soon as my feet felt the boardwalk surface. I grabbed the railing to steady myself as he ran back to the water and picked up his chair. He pushed it gingerly behind me so I could sit down and recover.

My teeth clattered together, and my hands quaked as anxiety wrapped around my neck, choking me.

"Ashley, what can I do?"
"It will pass in a few minutes," I said with a quivering voice.

People kept asking if we wanted help as they passed us by, and Ethan informed them I needed a minute. At least this attack didn't send my intestines into a frenzy like before. What an embarrassing mess that would have been.

Once my shaking ceased and allowed me to get up, I placed my palm on Ethan's arm.

"Thank you."
"I told you, whatever it takes," he said, smiling.

We padded along and stopped at several shops on our way back to my building. I found an adorable white doggie t-shirt with 'I woof Virginia Beach' in red letters for Ruger and a pair of round sunglasses for me.

Ethan bought only one thing from a pop-up shop, which creeped me out. He stared at the intricate details of the taxidermied mouse wearing glasses and holding a camera.

"Ethan, that's gross."
"What? He's cute. Look at his little camera," he said as he wiggled it in my face.

I shoved him away, and he chased me with it. It is the first time I have laughed about anything in some time. Tears came from laughter, not sadness, and I welcomed them as I panted before him, trying to catch my breath. As I moved closer to him, our eyes became fixed in a seductive stare.

"Put your hands behind your back and shut your eyes," I said.

He didn't ask any questions, and he did what I asked. Stretching my body upward, I kissed his smooth lips. His surprised face sprung to life as our tongues intertwined with each other. The intensity of our kiss sent a wave of emotions through me as the heat between us rose. It's too much, too fast. I pulled away from him, and he seized me with a loose grip.

"Ethan, I can't," I said, ripping my arms away from his.

"I'm sorry," he said as he sighed through his nose. "I miss you, Ashley."

I reached out to hold his elbow, and he offered it without a fight. We walked in silence back to my apartment, each with too much on our minds to say out loud. Patience is what I need right now. I only hope that he can stand by me long enough for us to reconnect like when we first met.

Chapter Twenty-Two – Sting

Over the last several days, Ethan took me to the ocean, used the fairytale, and carried me to the water. It became our new routine—a way to rebuild our relationship and my trust.

My slow progress weighed on him, so I tried something different today. Instead of him telling the story, I focused on his face with my eyes open. At first, panic gripped my throat, and I shook, but his tender words reassured me.

"It's me, Ashley. Look at me, nowhere else, just me," he said as his feet scurried over the grit.

It took several minutes for me to recover once he placed me in the chair. Words trapped themselves somewhere inside me like a caged animal as I tried to thank him.

"Don't talk. Just listen," Ethan said, pointing his finger to his right ear.

I sat silently, staring across the salty liquid at a boat heading out into the open water. In my younger years, my father would take me to his brother's yacht association, and we would cruise along the Erie Canal. I remember it being the most incredible thing I have ever experienced.

Being taught about canals in school and traveling through one is a unique moment that I can't forget.

My aunt would make me lettuce and mayonnaise sandwiches while the men hung out inside the club. One day, we tried our fishing and reeled in a carp. We threw it in the fridge to show the guys we, too, could be fishermen.

Once my father and uncle returned, they tossed it back in the canal and called it a 'garbage fish.' I thought we killed it by sticking it in the chiller, but it paused for a moment on the surface and swam away.

"What are you smiling about?" Ethan asked, resting his hand on mine to get my attention.

"A memory from childhood. My dad used to take me fishing," I said, taking my hand away and rubbing it.

"We can charter a boat if you're up for it."

"Sure, that sounds like fun," I said.

Ethan scooped me up and took me to the boardwalk. People probably assumed we were on our honeymoon because he carried me everywhere, but something more sinister kept my feet from touching the crushed quartz, trauma.

We made it to the ship just in time to catch the next tour. They supplied complimentary rods, which Ethan and I set up at the bow. I hooked one first and needed help to reel it in. Ethan stood behind me, and our bodies touched as he took the pole and wound the fish towards us.

The spotted sea trout is about twenty-four inches long and fought for its life as Ethan held it in front of me.

"Ethan, let it go."
"What? These are excellent to eat."
"It's my fish, I decide, and I want you to let her go, please."
"Her? Did you name it too?"
"Not yet," I said, crossing my arms and tapping my foot on the boat's sole.

He hung his head, untangled the scaley creature, and tossed it over the side. I smiled as it vanished into the deep, hoping it wouldn't retake the bait. Ethan snagged a sea bass after that and placed it in the cooler. He plans to make it for dinner later, which is his choice, but fish and I disagree.

A sizeable speedboat darted dangerously close to us, causing a sudden shift in my footing. I reached for the bow railing, but there was nothing, and I tumbled overboard. Ethan dove in after me as the vessel slowed to a stop. An orange and white circle with a rope attached sailed over me as Ethan swam in my direction.

Without warning, stinging needles stabbed me repeatedly. I flailed helplessly as a translucent jellyfish floated over my thigh.

My arms grasped desperately for the flotation device, but it shifted just out of reach with every attempt to grab it. Saltwater filled my throat and lungs as I struggled to stay above the surface. But the fire from the jellyfish's tentacles pulled me under, and my strength dwindled. Within seconds, I was under the waves for good, sinking into the deep sea. As the light above vanished into a greenish haze, my galloping heart slowed to a faint pulse.

Ethan swatted the jellyfish away with his bare hand and reached for me. He wrapped his arm around my chest, and with a powerful kick of his legs, we broke the surface.

He snatched the life preserver so the crew could pull us ashore. The welt made me think of pink yarn strewn across my leg as the captain poured an endless amount of white vinegar onto my swollen limb.

I gagged and puked on my lap as Ethan rubbed my back. The crew handed the captain a knife, and I pushed myself away from him.

"It's all right, ma'am. I need to scrape those stingers," he explained.

"Give it here," Ethan said, reaching for the sharp instrument.

He came before me, turned the blade on its side, and waited for me to give him permission. I nodded, and he scraped across the wound multiple times, then rinsed it with vinegar again. He repeated this twice. Then, applied a cream to it.

The stinging calmed to a tolerable level, and Ethan came and sat beside me. The tentacles spared no one in their wake, not even him. I grabbed the small amount of smelly solution that was left and dumped it on his hand.

"We need a shower," he said after several minutes of silence.
"That is a nasty sting, young lady. A doctor should treat it," one of the crew pointed out.
"Yes, sir," I said.

The gangway dropped for us to disembark, and a cab idled in the lot to take us to the hospital. Ethan's leg bounced beside me as the swelling around the area grew. As the driver pulled under the emergency room carport, I rested my hand on his knee to ease his worry.
When I stepped out of the backseat, I grabbed Ethan's arm. My head felt funny, and I couldn't walk straight.

"Ashley, what is it?"
"Ethan, something's wrong," I said as I lost my balance, and he caught me.
"Help us. She's reacting to a jellyfish," he screamed at the first person he met.

Ethan laid me on a stretcher they brought out to him, and his face disappeared around a corner as they rushed me into an available room. Hands ran from one side of me to the other as they fired questions at me so fast that I didn't have time to answer all of them.

"Ashley, how is your breathing?" The doctor asked, shining a light in my eyes. "Ethan said you feel dizzy and vomited as well. Is that right?"
"Yes. Can he hear me?"
"No, he is in the waiting room."
"I'm pregnant."
"Won't hurt a thing. The medicines we are using are all proven safe for expecting mothers. Ashley, does he know?"
"No, I don't want him to," I sighed.

A nurse handed him a chart, and he flipped through it, nodded to himself a few times, then gave it back to her.

"Well, your other lab work came back just fine, and the baby is growing."

Tears burst out of me like an alien in a movie, and the physician patted me on the shoulder.

"You're both going to be all right."

After loading me up with various medicines, they allowed Ethan to come in and sit with me. The doctor wants me to stay and be observed for a few hours, and then I can go home.

He kissed my cheek when he sat down, then kept his hands to himself for the rest of my stay. The nurse returned with my discharge instructions in a bag, and they called a ride for us to leave.

We giggled as the cab driver covered his nose with his shirt and bitched under his breath. As we drove past my earlier condominium, police vehicles surrounded the outside with their lights on.

"Sir, what is going on over there?" I asked.

"Yeah, some idiot tried to sneak into the building, and they called the cops when he got irate," he mumbled through his face cover.

The man pulled in front of my apartment, and Ethan jogged to my side to help me. I put my arm around his waist as he punched the codes to enter.

The multiple flights of stairs before me only bother me now. Usually, I would sprint up them and grab a quick burst of cardio, but I can't, not in my present condition.

"Ashley, I am going to pick you up, and we will do this one flight at a time. Okay?"

"Yes."

Ethan picked me up, took me to the first landing, and then set me back down. My legs wobbled, but I didn't fall as I braced myself against the wall until the nervousness passed. Once I relaxed, I went to him.

He moved slower this time, but I held his neck and wouldn't let go.

"Keep going," I said.
"Are you sure? Because I don't want to drop you. It is a long way down."
"Ethan, go."

His strength and sheer desire not to lose me to gravity made me love him more. While I typed in the code, he took a moment to catch his breath.

We both walked to the bathroom at the same time to wash.

"It's all right, go first. I can wait," Ethan said, turning the shower on.
"Join me."

He didn't hesitate and climbed in. We washed and rinsed our stench down the drain without touching each other. I missed his body, every inch of its perfection. My hands slid down his abdomen and captured his shaft. He reached for me, and I let go and backed away.

"Don't touch," I said, reminding him of the rules.

His palms pressed against the wall behind my head as I grabbed his manhood once more. Our tongues twisted around each other like two serpents during mating season. I needed him, but I was afraid, and my heart was pounding inside my head, so I pulled away from him.

I snatched my robe off the hanger and exited the bathroom. He followed me out, dripping water all over the floor. His unrelieved erection bounced up and down as he walked closer, and I put my hand up.

"Ethan, I can't. I wanted to, and I tried, but I can't. I'm sorry."

Turning without a word, he went to the bedroom. I thought he might take care of his problem alone, but he came out wearing pajamas. He sat on the couch, motioned for me to sit beside him, and turned on the television.

As a show of trust and gratitude, I leaned my bare, crying body against his as he covered my naked skin with a blanket and held me.

Chapter Twenty-Three- Unraveling

Ethan had to have brought me to bed after I passed out on the sofa. The quiet in the apartment made me wonder if he snuck away after I went to sleep, so I investigated.

My body didn't want to cooperate this morning, and my leg itched like crazy as I shuffled into the living room.

"Ethan?"

Silence. How could I blame him for leaving me after what I had done to us? I should have let him have my love and suffered the consequences of how it made me feel later. Now I'm alone again in this space, weeping like a child who lost their mother in a strange place.

"Ashley, what's the matter?"

Ethan was knelt in front of me when I opened my eyes to his voice. Instead of answering, I hugged him so tight that I almost knocked him over. He wrapped his arms around me and combed my unruly hair.

"I thought you left me," I said, weeping.
"I'm not going anywhere."

After he had aided me off the couch, he put plates on the table overlooking the ocean for us. He left to fetch us bagels for breakfast and buy me more orange juice, but he didn't want to wake me. His phone buzzed on the counter, and it was Mills again.

"Shouldn't you get that?"
"No, I'm not planning on it. Then she will know where we are. She can leave a message. Right now, why don't you throw some more clothes on, and we can eat," Ethan said, smiling.

I stared at my current outfit, realized I was still in my robe from the night before, and put on blue stretchy shorts and a t-shirt. Ethan waited for me outside with cortisone on the table.
When I sat down, he dabbed his lips with a napkin and crouched in front of me.

"You enjoy your food, and I'm going to put some cream on your thigh."

He squeezed a ribbon of ointment into his hand and stroked my skin. A breath caught in my chest as his fingers moved in a circular motion across my angry limb.
The shaking in my hands matched my stomach as he took his hand from my leg and rested it on my face.

"I love you, Ashley," Ethan said as he leaned forward and kissed me.
"I love you too."

His phone rang again on the table, and he silenced it. When he walked inside, I tapped the screen. Ethan had three missed calls from Mills.
I brought it in and placed it in front of him.

"Perhaps you should call her back. You can use my burner. What if it's about him?"
"Later. Right now, I have something for you," he said, turning around with a black velvet box.

He got on one knee before my gaping mouth and opened the velvety square. Inside, a beautiful princess-cut diamond sat upon a red silk display, and my mind raced as I panicked.
Ethan doesn't know I'm pregnant, and I didn't want him to know, but if I say no, I will break his heart. If I say yes, and he finds out I'm pregnant, he may never trust me again.
Thankfully, he gave me an out as he pitched his offer.

"You don't have to answer me now. Please wear it as a promise that someday you will be ready to say yes. Things have been difficult, but I'm never going to leave, and I want everyone to know you are mine," he said as he slid the ring on my left digit.
"Ethan, it is gorgeous."

He hugged me around the midsection while still on the floor, and I stiffened as my breaths became rapid. My body wants him, but my mind is interfering, and they are battling one another. His face sat too close to my love-making zone, and my clitoris quivered.

As if he felt it, too, he slid my bottoms to the tile and stuffed his face in between. My brain took a vacation as my desire decided for me, and I forced his head in for more. A small part of me regretted my actions as his hands gripped my waist with a forceful strength, keeping me from moving away.

His tongue flickered around my labia like strings on a guitar, and I needed him to give me all of him. I moved his head away, pushed him back, and walked into the bedroom. The least I could do after such a fantastic gift was try again.

His manhood sprang out of his pajama bottoms when he laid down. I slid a condom over his appendage and covered it with my lady parts. The control of being on top gave me the drive to continue moving up and down at my own pace in my own way. I felt pleasure for the first time in a long time, but it was short-lived.

Ethan grabbed my hips and flipped me over, wanting more. A flashback struck me like a smack to the head as he entered me from behind and thrust himself aggressively into me. My brain took me to that moment when the killer repeatedly rammed my body with this length.

Ethan had never been like this with me before, and I was unprepared for my reaction.

I screamed and bucked him off me like a wild mare trying to escape capture. He flew backward onto the floor and cracked his head on the dresser. A reddening knot formed on his forehead as he sprang to his feet and charged me.

"God dammit, Ashley," he yelled, stopping short in front of me.

"I'm sorry, baby," I cried, concealing my naked shame with a sheet.

He shoved his limbs into jeans, threw a top on, and stormed out of the house. I collapsed onto the bed and cried my eyes out. What is wrong with me? How can I long for something so bad and then freak out when it's given to me?

After running out of liquid grief, I switched on the television. The news came with a breaking report about the incident at my former complex.

'A journalist from North Carolina allegedly broke into a secure condominium and is being questioned by the FBI. The man claims to know who the Cavern Killer is and is being held in custody for the time being...'

Perhaps that is why Mills keeps calling Ethan to tell him about the reporter. I could be whom he came there for so I could contact him and find out.

That way, I could put a name to my kidnapper even if I didn't have a face to go with it. It was a good plan that I would work out tomorrow.

Right now, I have some making-up to do. If I cooked his favorite dinner, maybe he could forgive me for what happened.

He loves chicken stir-fry with snow peas, asparagus, and carrots. But I jazzed it up and used sweet and sour sauce instead of a traditional one. I made a list of items I needed to buy at the market, slid on Ethan's oversized sweatshirt, and headed to the store.

The woman at the checkout viewed me as though she knew who I was, and I avoided her stare. Finally, when she spoke, I was surprised at her question.

"Are you a famous supermodel? Because I feel like we have met before, or I have seen you in a magazine or something," she said, continuing to gawk.

"No, I'm not sorry."

"Well, you should be," the clerk said.

"Thanks."

She's seen me before because I survived an elusive murderer, that's why, but I held that tidbit to myself. An angry cloud hovered over the horizon, and even though the sky above my head was clear, rain dribbled upon it. I quickened my pace and hustled back to the apartment.

Still no Ethan. I may have scared him off, but I still stuck with the plan to prepare a meal for him.

My disposable phone rang as I dropped my reusable shopping bag on the ground, spilling its contents. It was Ethan, but he hung up before I could get to it. I tried him back, and when he didn't pick up, I assumed he had butt-dialed by mistake.

I continued taking care of groceries and preparing food as a storm raged on the other side of the glass. Leaves and paper blew onto the balcony from below as the wind carried them where it wanted.

A mighty thump slammed into my door, stopping me from cooking. The doorknob shifted back and forth as someone played with its knob. I grabbed a knife from the counter, walked over to it, and listened.

It rattled next to my head, and scraping fingernails scratched at its surface. Inaudible phrases came from the other side, but I didn't catch what they said. What if the reporter found me and was trying to break in? Holding the blade in my grasp, I ordered them to leave through the door.

"I'm calling the police if you don't get away from my door," I yelled.

"Ashleeeeeey," Ethan's voice said, trailing off. "Open up and let me in… open… in…."

I whipped the door open, and Ethan's rain-soaked drunken body fell in. This is the first time I have ever seen him drunk. He has consumed a drink or two before but has never been trashed. Is this what I drove him to?

This mess on the landing outside my apartment is my own doing. I took his arm when he reached for me and helped him. He glanced at the knife in my hand and tried to grab it.

"Were you going to stab me?" He said with slurred words.

"I thought about it," I sighed as I set the weapon on the kitchen counter.

We staggered to the bedroom, and I dropped his uncooperative figure on the bed. I removed his shoes, socks, and pants, then peeled his top off like excess skin. Ethan grabbed me around the waist, buried his face into my chest, and mumbled inaudible sentences.

"What did you say?" I said as I pulled his head away from my breasts.

"Sing for me..." he muttered as his arms became tight. "Siiiiiiiiing."

Chapter Twenty-Four – Expecting

The awkward pause between us lasted only seconds as I realized what Ethan had said, and so did he. He never meant to say it aloud or to me, but alcohol gave his silent, twisted mind a voice.

"Ethan, let go."
"Never…" he said, yanking my body back to him.

My hands turned to fists, and I punched him several times, but he was much bigger than me. Ethan gained control with little effort and pinned me to the mattress. His face came within an inch of mine, and he inhaled my scent.

"Why did you do this to me, Ethan?"
"Why? You're seriously going to ask me why? It's because it's what you wanted."
"What are you talking about? Ethan, you murdered those women, kidnapped me, and raped me. Why?"

He climbed off me and reached for something on the dresser.

"I thought those women were the ones too, but they would do something stupid I didn't like or couldn't change in them, so I got rid of them. But you are perfect, or at least I thought until I read this."

My diary struck me in the arm. After the incident in the cave, I never went back to writing in it, so I didn't realize it was missing. Ethan came toward me, and I jumped away from him as he swiped the journal off the bed.

"Let me read it for you."

'August 3

Ethan and I had sex last night. He took his time and only satisfied himself. I long for him to ravish my body and make more effort. I wish he would grab me and be rough about it for once. There is no excitement in our intimate moments, and I don't know how much longer I can take this boredom.'

"See, you asked for it. You wanted me to be more aggressive, but now that I have, I can't even touch you, so my plan clearly backfired. We can't even make it through sex, for God's sake," he shouted as he flailed his arms in the air and launched the private book across the room.
"Ethan, please tell me what you want."
"You," he hollered as he gripped my ankles, spread my legs, and tried to mount me.

My limbs thrashed as I screamed and kicked at him when he tried to gain control. One of my kicks landed in the center of his chest, knocking the wind out of him. I leaped out of bed and ran towards the front door, but his hand went around my neck as soon as I reached the knob. Ethan steered my head like a joystick as he directed me into the other room by my throat.

I slapped his arms wildly as he shoved my legs down onto the crème-colored area rug and pushed my head into the couch seat. Somehow, I broke free and made a mad dash for the exit.

My body flew into the door as he turned into a human barrier, blocking my escape. The door rattled as our bodies fought against it for different reasons.

Ethan snatched me by the hair, spun me around, and bent me over the kitchen counter. My stomach cramped, and my insides quivered. I cleared my mind, threw my head backward in a blood-curdling screaming rage, and struck Ethan in the nose. The knife on the granite protected me as I pointed it in his direction, keeping him back.

He stopped his advancement, only for a second, and then kept moving. I swiped the blade at his reaching hand, slicing it the long way down his palm. Guilt made me hesitate, which didn't end well as he seized my weapon-wielding wrist and took the only thing keeping him from me.

When I tried to flee, he put me in a headlock and stuck the sharp side of the instrument against my throat.

"Stop fighting, or I will kill you," he uttered, pressing the point into my skin and drawing blood.

"Ethan, I'm pregnant."

Ethan released his hold on me and stepped away, not expecting this turn of events. His eyes darted around the room as he searched for an explanation of what he had just heard. Then, his face turned dark.

"Liar," he yelled. "Why would you say such a thing? You know how much children mean to me."

"It's the truth. Check the bag from the hospital. My discharge instructions are inside."

He crossed the room, whipped the bag open, and threw the plastic onto the tile as he read. The papers floated to the floor as if gravity were in short supply, and tears cascaded over his cheekbones. Ethan moved toward me at a turtle's pace and touched my belly with his fingertips, stroking it.

My muscles recoiled at the vile intrusion of his hands of death, and I pulled myself further from his reach. His digits wiggled in the space between us as if they, too, were shocked by the news.

"I'm going to be a father?" He said as he reengaged them. "Boy or girl?"

My limbs shook as my frail heart shattered into pieces like a rock on a windshield. His voice turned into white noise, and my ears rang as I cautiously stepped further away from him.

"Ashley!" he shouted, slamming his fist on the counter. "Boy or girl?"
"Girl. I think it's a girl," I stuttered, startling away from him.
"A daughter. She will be beautiful, like her mother," he said as he forced me to accept his mandatory embrace.

The metallic scent from his hand near my face caused a surge of vomit to make its way into my mouth. I moved away from him at once and threw up in the sink. Gasping for air in between each heave, undigested pieces of bagel narrowed my airway on their way out.
Ethan massaged my back until I finished and handed me a towel. The minute he turned his back, I darted for the door, and he slammed his fist into the wall above my head when he caught me.

"You're not going anywhere. We have so many things to discuss, like our future, baby names, and expectations from now on," he said while stroking my cheek with his thumb.
"She has a name," I said, pushing back against his touch.
"Both parents should agree upon such an important decision, don't you think?"

"Not this time. Not after what you did to me," I hissed at him.

"Well, out with it so I can tell you how much I hate it," he pronounces as he waved the knife in front of my face.

"Aurora," I said as salty liquid sadness slid over my lip.

Ethan closed his eyes, envisioned the name on the face of our future offspring, and smiled.

"Auroooooooraaaaa. Yes, it's perfect. Excellent choice, my love. Come, let's clean up," he said, dragging me by the elbow into the bedroom.

Ethan stripped me of my stained clothing and lifted me into the tub. After washing us both from head to toe, he pinned me against the shower wall and warned me about the punishment if I didn't cooperate.

"If you try to leave or fight, I will keep you until our daughter is born, then kill you. Understand?"
"Ethan, don't do this."
"Understand?" he screamed in my face.
"Yes, I'm sorry. Please don't yell," I said, covering my tender ears.

Ethan kneeled before my soaked bare body and kissed my belly as he spoke to it.

"Hi baby girl, it's your daddy. I will take excellent care of you, with or without your mom's help. It's up to her," he explained in an ominous tone.

His breath chilled my collarbone as he rested his head on my shoulder and circled my tummy with his hand. My stomach twisted into knots as his fingers walked from my abdomen to my face. He wrapped his digits around my chin, and I pulled away. A quick slap across the face reminded me he was in charge as he retook it. As he caressed my reddening face and kissed me gingerly on the mouth, I didn't reciprocate, which angered him.

My defiance was met with a strike to my jaw from his palm, and this time, when he kissed me, I returned the favor. His tongue parted my lips as he made love to the interior of my mouth and then turned me around so he could take what he wished.

He entered me with finesse and careful movements, afraid to hurt our growing child. Finally getting the release he had been waiting for after so long, Ethan cried out as his fluids spilled inside me. He held me there, catching his breath while I sobbed.

The water changed to cold, and I made no motion to get out when he shut it off. He stepped onto the bathmat, reached out to me, and expected me to take his hand. But I was stuck, frozen where I stood, holding myself around the abdomen and wishing someone would come and save us.

After he hoisted me out of the tub, Ethan dressed me, packed a bag of clothes for each of us, and filled another with food.

As often as I tried to leave and subsequently failed, now I am afraid to as he forced me out of my apartment. My sneakers dug into the carpet as my body leaned away from the steps, and I held a death grip on the railing.

"Move your legs, Ashley," Ethan insisted as he squeezed his fingertips into my forearm.

I released it and took my time ascending the stairs. Becoming aggravated with my purposeful delay, he gripped me by the hair and whispered another haunting warning.

"Remember the rules, Ashley. Cooperate, and we can raise Aurora together as a family, or don't, and you can die never seeing her face. Am I clear?"

I nodded, and he let go, motioning me forward. The pounding inside my chest made it to my head, and I felt dizzy as we came closer to the bottom. The icepick-like pain in my temple stopped me, and Ethan dropped our bags. They tumbled down the last few steps, almost hitting the neighbor.

"Is she all right?" the young man asked.
"She's fine," Ethan said, shooting me a nasty stare.

"Ethan, my blood pressure," I said, grasping my thumping heart.

I flinched as his arms folded around me, and he placed his ear to my sternum. Ethan rubbed my ribs up and down with his hands, sighed, and pushed his glasses onto the bridge of his nose.

"Okay, I am going to pick you up. Don't freak out."

Ethan is my fiancé, Aurora's father, and a serial killer who raped me, so why would I freak out if he picked me up?
The young man on the landing grabbed our bags while Ethan carried me the rest of the way to his car.

"She appears pale. Maybe I should call for help," the man announced, pulling out his phone.
"No," Ethan yelled, smacking his telephone away.
"Well, that's uncalled for," he said, picking it back up. "Fine, I will call the police instead."

As soon as the words left my neighbor's lips, I knew Ethan would kill him. I shook my head at the man, trying to give him a hint of what was coming, but it was too late. He didn't stand a chance as Ethan stabbed him over and over. I screamed at him to stop, but it was as though he was on autopilot and had no control over his actions. The neighbor's

211

astonished face drifted to the harsh pavement in slow motion as Ethan stood over him.

The operator on the other end of the line asked if this was an emergency as Ethan flipped the deceased Good Samaritan's phone closed and threw it onto the bloody pavement.

He wiped the blade of his knife on a clean part of the dead body's shirt and slid into the driver's seat. The way he held the knife handle on his lap made me wonder if he was contemplating taking me out as well. He looked over my shattered face, glanced down at my tummy, and put the weapon back in the console.

I hyperventilated next to him as he reached over, latched my seatbelt, and covered my mouth with a wet cloth. The last thing I saw as I drifted into darkness was the empty eyes of a corpse.

Chapter Twenty-Five-The Dark Room

My heart leaped into my throat as I awakened in a pitch-black place. No light came from any direction as I peered around me. My cuffed left wrist clanked against something metal.

"Ethan?"

Footsteps creaked over my head, then stopped as though someone was listening.

Not wanting him to know, I was conscious, yet, I remained quiet. Using my feet, I rubbed the surface beneath me to get a sense of my surroundings. It feels like a mattress, maybe a twin. The furry blankets warmed my body and felt cozy, but I knew better. This is not for my benefit. This is for him.

After rotating to a sitting position, I waited for the dizziness to pass. Perhaps this is some cruel joke. Ethan can't possibly think he could keep me in this dungeon for the next eight months, could he? A light appeared behind me, and I pulled my legs back onto the bed. It provided enough illumination for me to see my environment.

As my eyes adjusted, the walls were so close to me that I could touch them on both sides. A chain ran from my handcuffed wrist to the space behind my head, where it hooked to a three-foot stainless steel bar.

I am not claustrophobic, but these tiny quarters gripped my abdomen with a violent shaking unlike any other. Soon the rest of me joined in the quaking, and my teeth chattered as I suffocated.

"Ethan," I yelled.

Keys jingled on the other side as it unlocked, and Ethan peered inside.

"You're awake. I've been waiting," he smiled, turning on the light.
"Ethan, where are we?" I asked, squinting at him.
"Well, right now, you are in an old storage closet, but don't worry, it's only temporary while I finish preparing your room."

He came and sat next to me on the bed. My legs folded into me, trying to keep their distance, but he snatched one and pulled it to him. The stroke of his hand unnerved me as he slid it back and forth on my uncovered skin with careful precision.
The room is entirely green, except for the floors, which are clean concrete. I think I may be in a basement, but I can't be sure. The secure door is the only way out. A single tear escaped my lid, and he swiped it with his pointer.

"Ashley, don't worry. This is temporary. Then I can move you next door. It is larger and has a window. I think you'll learn to love it," he smiled as he patted me on the thigh.

He stood up to leave, and part of me wished he would stay and tell me more. I needed to know his intentions, his plans for me, for us, but he didn't give me the opportunity to speak. The door slammed shut, and the dead bolt screeched into place. I'm not going anywhere.

The next room has a window. Perhaps that's my way out. If it's too small to climb through, I could still wave at people if they passed by. I know Ethan would never hurt Aurora, but what about me? I will live for now, but what about after she is born?

What if I make him angry, and he decides keeping me is more of a hassle than it's worth?

For now, I need to play nice and do everything he says until I produce a plan for our escape.

The door opened, and Ethan peeked inside.

"I put a bucket over there in case you have to throw up."

He closed the door fast, and there was no stopping my sadness. Tears poured out of me like rain through a downspout. I want to return to the way things were when I worked. Mr. Johnston could be an ass, but he cared about his employees when it mattered the most.

I worked hard for him, and he took notice when I no longer came to work. Ethan probably scared him off for good at my apartment. The attorney always seemed angrier with me than the others. Maybe there is something off about me.

Someday I may ask him.

The keys slapped against the door as he returned with a tray of food. I could eat everything on it with my hands, so he didn't give me any utensils. Peanut butter and jelly cut into four triangles, a bowl of strawberries, milk, and a bottle of water are what's for lunch or dinner.

"Ethan, can we please talk?"
"Later. Right now, I would like you to eat," he insisted.
"My stomach is upset."
"Eat!" he screamed.

I rested the sandwich on the plate after taking a small bite. He came over to me, placed his hand on my chin, and lifted it to face him.

"Good girl," he said before exiting.

At least he kept the light on so I could see while I picked at my meal. I only consumed one of the four pieces of my sandwich and a few strawberries before the heartburn started. The milk helped, but not for long.

My mouth filled with fluid, and vomit came right after. I grabbed the pail with my unrestrained hand and threw up in it multiple times. The mess inside the plastic container resembled berries and cream frozen yogurt, which made it that much worse. It was my favorite dessert, but not anymore.

In the middle of heaving, the door opened.

"See, aren't you glad I left the bucket for you?"

I nodded as I wiped the dribbled belly contents from my lower lip. He passed me a towel to wipe my face and then uncuffed my hand from the wall.

"Let's brush those teeth."

He took me down the hall with three closed doors. We stopped near the one on the right. It was an up-to-date restroom with high-end gold fixtures, a clawfoot tub, a double vanity, and red paisley wallpaper.

He gave me a fresh toothbrush out of the box and a tube of gentle, sensitive toothpaste. I scrubbed the nasty from my mouth and rinsed it well, then glanced at the toilet. I have to pee, but I don't want to use the bathroom in front of him despite doing it many times before.

"If you have to go, it's fine," he grinned as he lifted the top.

"Can I go by myself?"

"Come on, let's not be modest. We have used the restroom together before."

The cold seat startled me as I sat my buttocks on it and waited. Nothing happened. I couldn't go. There was just too much pressure. Ethan reached over and turned the faucet on, but it didn't help. I started crying. My bladder hurt, and begged for relief, but he wouldn't leave, so I could go.

"I can step out, but I want something first," he said, kneeling in front of me.
"What?"
"Kiss me," he whispered.

I leaned forward and gave him a quick peck on the forehead, and shied away from him.

"That is not acceptable. What I want is a deep, passionate one that your life depends on."

This time, I shut my eyes and pictured someone else's face to make the act more tolerable. My former boss, Mr. Johnston, is the only handsome man I would consider.
I grasped Ethan by his face with both hands and shoved my tongue into his mouth.
When I pulled my face away, Ethan's words stuttered off from his lips as though he, too, was experiencing his first kiss.

"Perfect."

He stood up from the tiled floor and had an erection that he didn't hide from me. It stuck out like a pole inside of a tent, holding the fabric far away from his loins. I thought he might not keep his word, but he did.

Finally, I released an entire day's worth of urine in one shot, then washed my hands and met Ethan in the hall.

He returned me to the place he had just removed me from. I didn't want to go in, but he moved me forward. His manhood needed addressing, and he was not going to do it himself.

"Get on your hands and knees," he ordered.
"Ethan, please don't."
"Ashley, do as I say."

I turned myself around and crouched on my palms, waiting. At first, he did nothing but stare at my body, then he rubbed my butt from behind and kissed each cheek while pulling down my undies.

"Before I begin, I thought you'd be interested in an article I read online about sex during pregnancy. Did you know that rough intercourse during early pregnancy is safe? Me neither. Last time I feared hurting our little girl, but now, well, you get the point," he announced as he made an aggressive entry.

He held my hips tight in his grasp as he thrust into me while I screamed for him to stop. My abdomen cramped, and my arms collapsed under me. He grasped a handful of my hair and pounded himself into me as I cried out in sheer agony. Putting his arms around me he pulled me upright, grabbed me around the neck, and came inside me. Fluids drained down onto the fluff underneath me, and in my mind, I prayed it was not red.

    Ethan kissed my weeping face, pulled up his pants, and left me where I lay to suffer in solitude.

Chapter Twenty-Six-Fractured

By the time the cramping ceased, Ethan returned to retrieve me and take me to my new living quarters. He pulled off the blanket I covered myself with and halted. His face changed to one of regret as he saw what was beneath me.

I didn't want to cry, but the sadness on his face struck me hard as he left the room and returned with a blindfold. He wrapped it around my eyes and secured it so tight that I thought my eyeballs would burst. Without warning, he unhooked me and hoisted me off the mattress.

His feet ascended stairs rapidly, and filtered light shined through my blinder. Cold chilled my flesh as he moved over an uneven surface outdoors and stopped long enough to set me down.

His car door beeped and clicked. He rested me in the passenger seat, strapped the seatbelt over my chest, and laid the seat all the way down flat. A surge of hot air blasted across my sparsely clothed body, and the fabric seats heated my frigid backside.

"Ethan, where are you taking me?"

"Hospital. I am only going to say this once. If you even hint that we are anything but concerned expecting parents, I will kill everyone around us. Are we clear?"

"Yes," I sobbed. "Ethan, is it bad?"

He didn't answer me, which made everything so much worse. My life would end if I lost Aurora, not only because of the loss of my first child but because he would have no reason to keep me alive.

We drove for what felt like hours before he removed the cover from my eyes. My new view comprised streetlights, buildings, and an occasional truck that sat high enough for me to see the driver.

As the vehicle came to a squealing halt, Ethan hopped out and ran to my side of the car. The hospital lobby bustled with the sick and injured, but none of them took priority over me after Ethan proclaimed my dire situation.

The nurse motioned him to come with her as he carried me in and placed me on a sheet-covered cushion.

"Tell me what is going on?" she asked, handing me a paper gown.

Ethan did all the talking. I didn't say a thing, as he explained we had rough sex, which he read was all right, and now I am bleeding. The nurse shook her head and sighed as she called for ultrasound to come to my room.

"A word of advice, young man, believe nothing you read on the internet," she advised as she stepped out of the room.

The technician rolled in the machine and helped me place my feet in stirrups. Ethan rubbed my arm as she prepped the wand for entry. I flinched away from her as she touched the skin of my vaginal opening and clamped my thighs closed.

"I'm sorry. I know this is not comfortable for anyone, but it is the only way to know what's going on," she said.
"Look at me, Ashley. Let her in," Ethan said as he pulled my legs apart.

I cried as she inserted the probe and fished around for signs of life. The girl exhaled and smiled as she turned the screen towards us.

"There she is. That tiny little circle right there is your baby. It is too early to measure an estimated due date, but I would say you're between three to five weeks."
"My baby girl," Ethan said, smiling at the blurb.
"The doctor will be in to speak to you both," she said as she packed up her things and left us.
"I am so sorry I hurt you. It won't happen again, I promise," Ethan said, kissing my bare belly.

He didn't mean to hurt Aurora, but I am fair game to him, so I need to mind. I cried to myself as Ethan flipped through the television stations while we waited for the physician to make her appearance.

The obstetrician swooped into the room and lit into Ethan as if she were scolding a child.

Ethan shrank in the chair as she berated him for being so reckless as to take advice from the internet as opposed to speaking to a qualified professional. Inside, I smiled as he couldn't react to her condescending tone.

After she handed me strict bed rest instructions, she glared at Ethan and gave him a nasty reminder.

"Be kind to her insides. They're not a piece of meat you can tenderize."

I stifled a giggle at her choice of words, not intending to make fun. But Ethan took it that way as he grabbed me by the throat once we were back in the car.

"Do you think this is funny?" he said as he squeezed a little tighter.

I rubbed my abdomen, reminding him that the air he kept me from breathing also took away from her. He let go, put the white and black bandana back over my eyes, and drove off.

The radio played a song that I knew, and I sang. He would forgive everything with the gift I am sharing with him now. At least, that is what I hoped.

The car slowed to a stop, and I sensed his eyes on me. Air pushed in and out through his nose as he stayed quiet beside me until my lips fell silent. He didn't turn the music back on, and we drove the rest of the way to his lair without another word.

He shifted into park and allowed me to walk in on my own while he guided me. We walked up three steps, across a hollow-sounding porch, and inside a door that he locked behind us.

The floor changed from carpet to a hard surface, then turned into stairs. More carpet greeted my feet at the bottom, which threw me off. Are we somewhere else?

We made another turn and descended another set of steps, and the concrete ground returned. Another lock clicked as he removed the fabric from my eyes. The door we stood before differed from the others. I turned to Ethan, who had an excited grin on his face.

"Your room awaits you," he said, throwing the door open for the reveal.

Inside the vast room, a gigantic king-sized bed with curtains on the wall behind it sat across from us. To the left, a small dinette with two placemats waited for their next meal, and to my right, a dresser with a gold-trimmed mirror.

On the other walls, photographs of us at different stages of our relationship reminded me of the love we once shared.

"The restroom is over here," Ethan said, pointing behind me and to the right.

The Victorian-style bathroom is painted a beautiful shade of emerald with a clawfoot tub on the far wall and a gold and crystal chandelier hung above it.

The vanities, curved golden hardware, and plush white luxury towels added to the high-end ambiance of the space. I glanced down at the old-world patterned tiles and smiled, but my happiness crumbled as I remembered where I was.

I am not in some fancy hotel. This is my prison for the foreseeable future, made to appear elegant to aid in my comfort until the birth of our child.

Ethan came to me and hugged me from behind. I reciprocated the attention for safety's sake and placed my hands around his.

"It's so beautiful," I said, smiling.

The soft carpet curled in between my toes as I forced myself to be compliant and approve of his every move and offering. In the upper left-hand corner of the room, a blinking red light caught my eye as he moved toward the exit.

"It is off for now, but when I go, I will turn it on."

"Ethan, wait. Why can't I come with you? I promise I'll behave. Please don't leave me down here. What if there is a fire?"

"Then I will come to rescue you," he said, pointing to the camera.

As soon as the door shut, I ran to the bed and leaped on it. When I threw back the curtains, only a picture of a window with a view of the mountains sat on the other side.

There was a window, so he didn't lie. It's just not real. I am still in a closed-off room with no access to leave except the way we came in. Three solid, locked doors stood between us and our freedom.

Rage overwhelmed me as I leered at the false hope hanging on the wall. I ripped it down and smashed it on the corner of the brass bedpost over and over until it fell apart in my hands.

An enormous piece of glass sat by my distraught limb, so I picked it up and stared at it for an exceptionally long time. If I didn't have more than my own life to worry about, I would have slashed myself from my wrist to the crook of my elbow. A jagged, deep line that even the best of surgeons couldn't repair to save me.

But my Aurora deserves a chance at life, with or without me, so I set it back down as blood dripped from the cut on my hand, tarnishing its clean surface.

Chapter Twenty-Seven – New Plan

After my tantrum, Ethan came into the room and sat on the rug before me. He lifted my stained hand and examined the oozing wound.

"What have you done to yourself, Ashley? Come into the bathroom so I can wash it."

The bloody water swirled down the drain as he rinsed the injury and patted it dry with a towel, staining it. He glared at the red circle on his clean towel and threw it angrily to the ground.

An aggressive amount of ointment beaded onto my hand, and he wrapped it several times with gauze. His nose huffing became more rapid, and his eyes burned through me as he finished taping my palm.

Ethan grabbed my neck, steered me out of the restroom and back to the shoebox bedroom.

"We can talk about what just happened at dinner."
"Ethan, I am sorry. Don't leave me in here."

The door slammed in my face without another word from him. I scanned the room, but there were no holes, no other doors, and no windows. The only means of escape appeared to be the door, so I lay on the bed and stared at the ceiling.

The room swirled around me in a matter of seconds as I fixed my eyes on the polka-dotted drop tiles above me. I peered into the four corners of the room, looking for cameras, but none existed. If the space is vast enough and carried into the hallway, I can get out of this room.

I had no intentions of making my move until I knew for sure how far my idea could take me. Like a game of chess, I need to use strategy and think ahead to check this bastard. I steadied myself on the unsupportive mattress and pushed the tile above me.

Cobwebs and dust stood between me and about two and a half feet of extra space. Pipes for water and gas ran in different directions, but not enough to prevent me from crawling from one room and dropping into the next.

Jingling keys rattled outside the door, and I released the square into its rightful place. Crumbs littered the blanket beneath me, and I swiped them off just in time. Ethan opened the door just as I finished straightening up the comforter and making it neat.

"Dinner," he said, looking around the room.

When I entered the hall, I only moved my eyes upward and not my head as he walked behind me. The tiles in the hallway mimicked those of the room I had just left, and my new living space had them as well.

The stairwell door is at the opposite end, so the only way to know if that was the same is if he took me back to the tiny room. I must get into trouble, despite the consequences.

Ethan made a hearty salad with grilled chicken on top and my favorite dressing. I needed my strength if I intended to save us, so I ate as though my life depended on it.

"Someone's hungry," he said, staring at my empty plate.

"Guess so."

"Ashley, what would you have done if an actual window was above the bed?"

"I just wanted to know where we are," I said, dancing around the truth.

Ethan knows I am not the type of person to spew lies, so he pressed further and asked a more direct question.

"Were you planning to escape?" Ethan asked as he shoved a ranch-covered tomato into his mouth.

If I said yes, I would be punished, but if I lied, he wouldn't believe anything I said in the future. Needing to stay ahead of the game, I answered honestly.

"Yes," I said, twirling my plastic fork in my fingers.

A powerful smack across the head took away my hearing on one side as I toppled to the area rug. I crab-walked rapidly away from him as he came and stood over me. Ethan grabbed me by the front of my t-shirt and slapped my mouth, giving me a bloody lip. His face reddened with anger, and his eyes darkened underneath them as he transformed into a monster.

Tears poured from both sides of my face, and I quaked beneath him as he pinned me to the floor and touched his nose to mine.

"Listen, my love. I am the only person who can take you out of here. The only way this will end if you continue to break the rules is with me killing you. I want Aurora to have you in her life, but if this continues, you're replaceable," Ethan explained as he smeared the blood from my face.

"I'm sorry."

"In the end, sorry won't save you," he said as he gripped my wrist like a vise and led me back to the dungeon.

The ceiling is the same all the way to the locked metal door at the end. My method only cost me a few bruises and a fat lip, but it worked. Now I must convince him to take me upstairs.

I need to play by the rules and earn his trust by doing what he says going forward.

As much as I don't want to be around him, I will do what needs to be done to accomplish my goal.

Ethan didn't come back for hours. When he let me out, he appeared freshly showered and in his pajamas. He took me gingerly by the hand and swung our limbs as we reentered my living quarters.

On the bed, a red silk nightgown lay across its fluffy white surface with a matching pair of lace underwear.

"Change," he said, handing me the attire.

I peeled off my top and bottoms, then stood naked before him without dressing. What would be the point? Not willing to accept me bare, he picked the sparse fabric up and handed it to me. I put them on, and he motioned for me to lie on the bed.

Behind him sat his camera. He removed his clothing, only leaving the silk boxers he wore underneath. After setting the camera timer, he climbed on the bed beside me.

"Sit on my lap," he ordered.

I did as he requested as he pulled the back of my gown up, revealing the lace thong to the camera. Bursts of noise came from the device as it took multiple photos of us as Ethan changed me from one position to another. The final few shots were of him holding me around the throat as he entered me from behind.

Ethan's movements were quick but not pounding as before. I couldn't breathe as he squeezed my airway and came inside me.

His hand moved between my legs as he blended our juices together with his fingers and inhaled their combined scent.

"We smell so lovely," he said. "Smile for the camera."

I tried my best to manifest a genuine smile, but under the circumstances, it came out looking forced. Ethan scrolled through the images, smiling and pointing at them as he showed me. A captivating photograph caught his attention, and he sighed.

"This one. This is my favorite."

The image is of him taking me from behind with his hand around my throat as a tear slid down my cheek. My entire face was discolored from lack of oxygen and bruising. Inside my head, I wondered if he had taken similar images of the women he's already killed.

He climbed off the bed, put his pants back on, and left the room. I curled into a ball and cried until my tears ran dry.

Now that I look back on things, I feel foolish. The signs were all there, but I ignored them. The way he beat my boss, how he glared at me when things didn't go his way, and his annoyance with having to switch to fruity gum because mint triggered an emotional response. Red flag after red flag right in front of my eyes, but it was Ethan, harmless, camera-loving Ethan. How could I have been so naïve?

Playing house with him might break me in the end, but it will be worth it if he lets me live.

Chapter Twenty-Eight-Pattern

Some days I don't see Ethan all day long, but he comes in the morning faithfully, switches the picture on the wall behind my head, and we have breakfast together. I don't mind breakfast, but the constant twice-a-day photo changes got old fast.

In the evening, he would place an enormous image of the stars with a crescent moon dangling over a mountain. At the beginning of the day, he would switch it to sunrise, the same scene at different times of the day. It didn't make being trapped in this windowless room any more tolerable.

The timing of his visits matched up with working on a schedule. Occasionally, he would stay the night with me, but only if he wanted sex or someone to hold.

Ethan talks to Aurora every morning as if she can hear him. I flinch less now, and my level of comfort is returning.

Today, when he gazed at me, I stroked his hair and smiled at how he talked to my tummy. Every day I let him in a little more, and am less resistant, hoping it would earn me a field trip beyond these walls.

"You look happy."
"Of course I am. I'm going to be a father," he said, kissing my abdomen. "Hungry?"
"Starving."

"Excellent. I made Belgian waffles," Ethan said, removing the nighttime wall hanging.

"Ethan, can we stop switching the art every day? It doesn't make a difference."

Ethan slid his glasses up onto his nose and cleared his throat. My hands and legs shook as I backed away from him as he approached me with an ominous look.

"When I was younger, my mother would bring me down here to keep me safe. Sometimes, I would be down here for days at a time, and she would sneak me food. My father, as you know, was a mean drunk and would go on these benders. She took pictures of our yard, the sky, and random people. There were stacks of them, and I would go through them to pass the time. One day, she started screaming for help. I opened the door, and she ran towards me. Mother knew what he would do if he caught us both. So, she locked the door and told me not to open it, no matter what. So, I did. Instead of helping her, I sat in here like a coward while he beat her to death. Her blood crept under the door onto my fingers, and I listened as she took her final gurgling breath. When I tried to leave the room, I discovered that dear old dad had added an exterior padlock. My father left me down here with nothing to eat, no lights, nothing. After a few days, my mother's employer reported her missing, and the police came to do a wellness check. They found my father dead in his chair with a bullet to the brain. My life never returned to normal after that," he said, wiping his eyes.

"Ethan, I am so sorry."

"Well, you should be grateful for what you have. At least you have a toilet, a lamp, a bed, and food. What did I have? Nothing. So, for you to tell me the pictures don't help, well, you're wrong because they helped me."

Ethan left me and didn't come back to prove a point. Not having any food kept me from having heartburn or throwing up, which was pleasant, but I must eat for Aurora's sake.

I snooped through the shelves of the bookcase in my room and flipped open a cardboard box. Inside sat piles of photos of all different sizes and subjects, secured with rubber bands. These must have been what Ethan's mom brought to him.

I grabbed a handful and started looking at them for clues. His mother was a beautiful woman with hair like mine, and a hint of sadness sat behind her smile.

In some of them, she has bruises on her face, and so does Ethan. Only one image of Ethan's father existed in the stack from his time in the army. He told me once that his father killed many people overseas and didn't return the same man. I guess he wasn't the only man in the family born to kill.

One photo was of a tri-level home. On the far-right side, it has a basement and first and second floors. On the left, there was only one floor, plus the basement. Another photo appeared to be the back of the house, which showed a walk-out patio to the backyard. The front and backside have windows near the ground, yet I have none.

It can only mean one thing, that my dungeon is in a sub-basement.

Built to protect homeowners from bomb fallout or tornados, they are submerged underground.

I need to gain access to the level above me so I can escape through the sliding door. First, I must figure out what's at the top of the stairs at the end of the hallway. Is it another metal door or household one that's easy to break through or jimmy the lock?

The floor creaked over me, and Ethan came into the room within seconds. I thought he would be mad at me for having gone through his things, but he wasn't. He smiled, sat next to me on the bed, and picked up the picture of his mother.

"I miss her," he said, putting the photo back in the box.

"Ethan, I'm sorry. The pictures help," I said, placing my hand on his.

He stared at our hands for a moment, then took his away and continued picking up the photographs. After he returned them to the shelf, he reached for me to stand, but when I tried, I fell back over. My vision blurred, and I started sweating from every orifice.

"Ashley, what's wrong?"
"Blood sugar. I need orange juice."

Ethan ran out of the room without locking the door and took the steps quickly. Now would have been an opportune time to run, but my vision needed to be clearer, or I wouldn't make it far.
   I made no move to take the glass when he kneeled before me. So, he put it to my lips, and I gulped it.

"Fuck. I'm sorry. Will it hurt Aurora?"
"It can affect her mental function if it happens a lot."
"Dammit. Daddy's sorry, baby girl. I am going to make you a fancy dinner," Ethan said to my unresponsive torso.

This time, when he left, he locked the door behind him.
   In my mind, I thought about a timeline for my departure. I couldn't wait until my belly grew too vast. Otherwise, I wouldn't be able to climb through the ceiling. The other problem was getting through the second door. If it's metal with a slide bolt, I won't be able to breach it.
   Faking a hypoglycemic episode might work if he responds the same. Both ideas could work, but I needed a solid one. The latter option carries the greatest risk. If Ethan works most days, it would be the best time to leave without him noticing.

Keys rattled against the door, and Ethan came inside with a tray. On the menu tonight is fat-trimmed strip steak with mashed potatoes, a pat of butter, and broccoli. On the side sat a bottle of multivitamins, a glass of milk, and water with lemon.

When I swallowed the vitamin, I thought it echoed when it reached the bottom of my empty internal tank.

Ethan's hand slapped down onto mine when I picked up the serrated knife to cut my meat. I moved my hand away. He took the blade, snatched my plate, and sliced my food into bite-size pieces.

"Thank you, Ethan."
"You're welcome."

We ate in solitude with an occasional glance in one another's direction. I missed whom we used to be, though it could have been better. If he hadn't turned out to be a serial killer, I might have made it work.

"Dinner was delicious."
"I did my best," Ethan sighed as he cleaned up the table.
"Ethan, will you stay with me tonight?"
"Ashley, I have to wash dishes."

When he focused on me and my seductive eyes, he set the plates down and turned to me. I pulled his

242

pants down to his ankles, underwear, and all, and pushed him into the chair behind him. His shaft sprang to life as I removed all my clothes and mounted his rock-hard pleasure stick.

My mind raced as I forced myself to please him, as I had never done before. I thought about my boss's face and imagined we were having an illicit affair.

This is my purpose now, to serve him to save us. A mother will go to any lengths to protect her child, including making love to a killer. Aurora is who matters now, no one else.

My eyes popped open as Ethan's head buried into my breasts, and I gripped his hair. I pulled it hard as I thought about how things would be if he were captured or I escaped. If he lives, he will get to us, even from prison.

As he erupted inside me, I realized I had already decided.

Ethan must die, whether by my hand or someone else's; his existence is not an option. Aurora never needs to know who her father is. I plan on making sure of it.

I panted on his thighs as he breathed heavily in front of me, then I took him by the face, kissing him deeply.

"I love you, Ethan. Regardless of what you have done, I will always love you," I said as I climbed off his lap and cried.

He stared at his lap as though he was debating whether he still loved me, got up, and left without his clothes. A telling sign that he, too, is struggling.

It is one thing to be born or bred a killer, but it is another to become one to save your own life. He may hold all the cards now, but I am playing the long game and thinking ahead.

Though I bear the resemblance of a sacrificial pawn, I will trap this king and win this match. The only exception is that there will be no threats, no capture, no protection, only death.

Chapter Twenty-Nine Separation

The sugar episode worked against me. Ethan carried in a tote of food and set it on the table. Inside are bottles of orange juice, fat-free gummy bears, honey pouches, and individual servings of applesauce.

In the center of the dinette, he placed a split bowl with apples on one half and grapes on the other. Ethan had created a new rule.

"In the future, while you're awake, you must eat something every two hours. No exceptions. I will not have my daughter come out with mental issues because you didn't manage your diet."

"Ethan, I would do nothing to harm our baby. You left me down here with no food, remember?"

"I made a mistake, and now that I have read up on the subject, I plan on making sure there are no further incidents," he said as he glanced at his watch.

An alarm rang over my head as though it came from a mall intercom somewhere. I jumped and turned in a circle to find where it was coming from. It was way too loud and annoying, so I covered my ears. Ethan fiddled with his phone, and it decreased to a tolerable but still irritating level.

"Ethan, what is that?"

"That, dear, is your reminder. Every two hours, it will go off, and you need to eat or drink something from the table or the box. I don't care which. It's your decision," he said as he prepared to leave the room.

"But what if I am sick or not hungry?"

"Eat!" Ethan screamed as the door closed. "I will be watching you."

"Wait, when? Does it start now because it just rang, or was that a test?"

"Now, Ashley. Right now," he sighed as he locked the door.

I peered up at the camera with its green light flashing, grabbed a handful of grapes, and stuffed them in my mouth. It is becoming more like a prison every day. What's next? Is he going to watch my bowel movements?

After taking a hot shower, I rearranged things. If I am stuck here, the least I can do is make it comfortable. The bed's location is practical but not esthetically pleasing, so I tried to move it, but it didn't budge.

I glanced underneath and raised my eyebrows. The legs are bolted to the floor. The metal headboard also had brackets to keep it from striking the wall with movement.

But that wasn't all I noticed. As I traced the headboard to the area below the mattress, an attached handcuff sat unused with the help of

Velcro. I scurried over to the other side, and it had one, too. The footboard was different. It had fabric buckle cuffs, and they were tucked under the bed.

All of them are new, so I know he bought them for me, but why? I can't leave this room. There is no means of escape. Why feel the need to strap me down?

My heart pounded, and my stomach shivered as my mind came to a startling conclusion. This is for when I give birth to Aurora.

I ran to the bathroom and emptied my intestines all at once. Does he think he can deliver Aurora on his own? What if something goes wrong? Will he cut me open like a savage from medieval times? I grabbed the wastebasket beside me and started throwing up. Shredded grapes and orange juice from this morning shot through my nose and mouth, burning them.

Chills scattered across every surface of my skin as a full-blown anxiety attack took over. Ethan appeared in front of me with his shirt over his face. He flushed the toilet, turned on the shower, and placed me inside. He removed the handheld showerhead and washed my body. The shaking wouldn't stop, and my teeth chattered noisily.

After thoroughly drying me, he lifted me out of the tub and carried me to bed.

"Ashley, look at me. Focus on your breathing. In and out like this," he said as he took a deep breath and released it. "Close your eyes and think of

Aurora. What is she doing? What are her features? Keep breathing."

I held my eyes closed and envisioned my baby. Aurora's hair is just as red as mine, with eyes as blue as the summer sky. She's dancing around me as her freckled cheeks giggle with contagious laughter. I want to hold her and be in that moment with her. My eyes filled with tears as the anxiety retreated into its hiding place.

When I opened my eyes, Ethan was gone. I focused so hard on my thoughts that I didn't know he had left. Within seconds, Ethan came back carrying something hot in a coffee cup. I sat up in bed and took it from him.

"What is it?" I asked as the scent drifted into my sinuses.

"Chamomile and green tea."

"Thank you," I said, taking a sip.

He stayed with me until I finished and took the glass from me. I've had a few anxiety attacks in the past that he has helped me get through, but this one is different.

This was because of him, not some outsider, not from my job, or having a bad day. I know he saw me find the restraints and the reaction that followed. Why else would he have appeared by my side so fast?

Ethan shifted his glasses, stood beside the bed, and reached for my hand.

"Come with me. I want to show you something."

I clenched his hand and took my time standing, as my legs were still unsteady. He walked me towards the door and unlocked it. We headed straight for the door at the end of the hallway, and he opened it. I'm going upstairs, and he isn't blindfolding me, so our trip must be limited to the bowels of his den.

The door at the top of the steps is wood, but something is different. As we crossed the threshold, I peered over my shoulder, and the entrance was a bookcase. If anyone dropped by, they would never know it was there. Across from the passageway, the sliding glass door leads to the yard.

Ethan took me up another flight of stairs where a fourth door didn't have a lock and stood open. This door led to the kitchen. The house seemed smaller than in the pictures, as if part of it was missing. Perhaps there was a fire in one half, and they rebuilt it to create a new flow.

We continued down a short hallway, passing a small bedroom on one side and a bathroom on the other. In the end, Ethan stopped in front of the last room and smiled.

"Shut your eyes," he said with a grin.

I did as he asked, and he guided me forward. My stomach tensed with uncertainty as he ended my advancement and held me around my waist.

"Open your eyes, Ashley."

Ethan has set up Aurora's nursery. A bright white crib sat on one wall with a sheer light pink canopy hanging above it. The other wall has a changing table and dresser. A rocking chair sits in the corner with a rose-pink cushion for comfort. When he turned me around and opened the closet, purchase tags dangled from an array of newborn clothes.

I took his arm away from me so I could explore the room on my own. The chair comforted me as I sat down and stared out the open window. No neighbors were in sight from this vantage point, so no one would see me.

"Check this out," Ethan said, pulling a box out of the back of the closet.

It was a multifunctional stroller and car seat set. I loved the color he chose. It was coral pink instead of traditional, and the stroller resembled a buggy.

"Ethan, I love it. You did an amazing job. I wish you would have let me help," I said, getting up and walking to the crib.

"Well then, it wouldn't have been a surprise."

Inside the crib, a pink elephant with 'Aurora' on the front smiled at me. Above it was a single framed photograph of my belly with a red heart drawn on it. Inside, our baby girl's name is spelled out in the middle.

"Ethan, when did you take this?"

"When you first got here," he said as he interlocked his fingers around my abdomen. "Do you like it?"

"I love it," I said as my grip tightened on the crib railing.

"I can't wait until she's here. I'm going to take her for walks and to the park. I even bought one of those baby things to strap her to my chest."

My knuckles whitened with anger, and my eye started twitching. All I have heard from him in the last several minutes is I, I, and more I. There was no 'we' or 'us' mentioned, just himself.

I am not the only one who has decided about my fate. Ethan intends to kill me and has fantasized about his life with our baby girl without me in it. Although I stand before him with a joyous smile, inside, I am screaming. If he could see behind my eyes and the sinister smile lingering there, he would know that my future wasn't the only one in jeopardy.

Chapter Thirty – Power

Ethan didn't let me visit the nursery for long, but it was all I needed to devise a plan. That hidden door swung into the room and not towards the stairs. This design is so that if you lean on it and it is unlatched, you wouldn't tumble down the steps.

It was never meant to hold a person captive. The entry latch is to my benefit and will be easy to pry open. I must find something like a credit card somewhere in my makeshift house.

A plastic knife would do the trick, but Ethan removes anything that could be used as a weapon against him.

I stared at the box of photographs sitting on the shelf. Some images were polaroid, so their rigidity could work, but they were flimsy and would need to be a little stronger. If I glue a few together, it might be strong enough to wedge between the door and the frame.

Now the hard part is making the adhesive. I need sugar, water, and flour. I have two of the three on hand, but flour will be hard to get my hands on.

The lights flickered as a crack of thunder vibrated the ceiling above me. It's storming outside, and it sounds like a nasty one.

I peered around the room, looking for ideas when two drywall seams caught my attention. They bothered me because they were not flush with the wall, and the screws holding them were drawn in too tight.

The inside of the drywall has a chalk consistency which would make an excellent substitute for flour.

Without warning, the lights went out, and the camera in the corner changed to a blinking red. Feet stomped across the floor above me as Ethan made his way downstairs. A generator started supplying partial energy, but his security was offline.

He threw the door open and huffed his way to the corner.

"Is everything all right?"

"No, Ashley, it's not. I was in the middle of a crucial meeting," Ethan said as he worked to get his equipment rebooted.

This is my way out. Storms take power out all the time. Even with the generator, you still must reset the cameras manually. All I need is one storm while he is away at work, and I can escape.

The camera went from red to blinking blue as it reset, then to green again. Ethan put his phone away, grabbed an apple off the table, and placed it in my palm.

"Eat. I will be back later."
"Thank you, Ethan."

He paused long enough in front of me for me to sneak in a reassuring kiss. I wanted to grab him by the nuts and rip them off his body, but it was not time yet. As I pulled myself away, he grabbed me by both arms and jolted me back to him.

"I don't know what little game you are trying to play with me, but I want you to stop. If I want a kiss or more from you, I will ask for it or take it. Don't mess with me, Ashley. It won't end well for you," he explained as he released his grip and locked me in.

He knows. Perhaps not the complete plan, but he can tell I have something up my sleeve. I need to take a step back and be more careful.
After finishing half of my apple, I took a broom, swept the floor, and purposely struck the bent-out drywall. A chunk of chalky material fell out and tumbled across the ground.
The trashcan closest is in the bathroom, so he wouldn't think anything of it if I poured the dustpan in there.
I took the chalk and rested it on a pipe beneath the sink. The toilet will supply water, so all that is left is a packet of sugar and a few polaroids.
A loud crash came from above, followed by a ruckus. Muffled voices penetrated the floor as the commotion persisted. Repeated thumps struck the ground over and over as though someone was bouncing a heavy ball against it. Then it fell silent.
My door screeched open, and Ethan came inside with blood on his face. I knew right then that

whoever came knocking was now dead. He looks so angry, I want to ask him what happened, but I fear the repercussions. Any normal person would want to know, so it is not like it's a dumb question.

"Ethan, what happened?"

I blurted the question out before my brain had time to stop me and regretted it right away. How he looked at me sent chills across my skin, raising the hair across every surface. I should have stayed quiet.

The pit in my stomach grew to the size of a small city as he approached me, and I took a few steps back.

"Get on the bed," he said, pushing me back.

My pulse leaped from my neck as he seized my wrists and attached me to the headboard. Then he grabbed my ankles and secured them to the end.

"Ethan, please. What did I do?"

Without a word, he ripped a piece of duct tape with his teeth, slapped it over my mouth, and walked out. The door stood open, and there was nothing I could do. His footsteps creaked above me, followed by the distinct sound of dragging. He's coming down the stairs with it.

Thump, thump, thump until he reaches the bottom. He panted outside my room for several minutes before finally entering and approaching me.

"I need to use your bathroom, but don't get upset," he said as he placed his bloody hand on my tummy. "The reporter stopped by. He knew who the Cavern Killer was, after all. Too bad he will never tell the story of how he figured it out."

He kissed me on the forehead and walked back out into the hall as my eyes filled with tears.

The dragging returned as Ethan slid the reporter through my open door by his ankles. His face no longer existed, just mush—a bloody trail smeared from the hallway to the bathroom. Ethan grunted as he hoisted the man up and dropped him into my tub.

My breaths quickened as Ethan hummed while sawing the dead man into pieces and placing them in bags. I am sure that using an electric saw this time was more convenient.

In the cave, he couldn't make too much noise, or he would attract attention. Once he finished dismantling the man like an old piece of furniture, he carried the bags away.

Above me, the swooshing sound of the floor being scrubbed started but didn't last long. A sudden drop landed in my hair, followed by another one. Bleach. It's oozing through the cracks and dripping onto my head.

I moved my head as far away as possible, but it was coming down faster. The smell nauseated me, but I couldn't throw up through my mouth, so it burst through my nose instead.

My body flopped up and down, trying to change positions, but I was strapped to all four corners. All I could do was turn my head to one side to stop myself from drowning. Everything burned inside me as I swallowed some of it back down and retched again.

Ethan ran to my side, yanked the tape off, and unhooked my right wrist and ankle. He turned me onto my side and rubbed my back as I puked into the trash can he held under my mouth.

"I'm sorry. I didn't realize the bleach had come through. Look what I did to your hair," he said as he twirled a discolored piece. "After I finish cleaning the shower, we will wash your hair."

I vomited again. The thought of him showering me in there ever again made me sick. How can I get over this?

He unhooked me from the restraints and took me into the clean restroom, but he used bleach there too. Moisture forced its way into my mouth, and I threw the toilet lid open and hurled into it.

Ethan turned the fan on, but it didn't help. I leaned my body against the side of the tub to catch my breath and rest. Something caught my eye behind the toilet.

I tilted myself further forward to see and crawled away from it at once. The tip of a finger from the knuckle to the fingernail rested on the shut-off valves washer.

"Ashley, what's wrong?"

"Ethan, you missed something," I said, pointing with a shaking hand.

"Thank you for letting me know," he said as he dropped it nonchalantly into the toilet and flushed.

The appendage swirled in a circle and went out of sight. Ethan sighed over me, reached down, grabbed me under the pits, and helped me to my feet.

He let me wash alone and dried me when I exited. I slipped on my house shoes and shuffled over to the bed. Circles of bleach discolored the sheets in different sizes, ruining them. The ceiling still dripped on and off, so I couldn't lie down.

I sat at the table, put my head down on my folded arms, and sobbed. I'm so tired of everything. I want it to be over. Snot and tears spilled onto the table as Ethan approached me and placed his hand on my thigh.

He positioned himself so his eyes lined up with mine, and a part of me could see that he still cared. I turned my body toward him and hugged him as though he meant the world to me.

"I'm sorry, Ashley," he said as he stroked my hair and held me before leaving.

Although my heart breaks for the dead man Ethan killed, someone will report him missing. The police and FBI already questioned the reporter, so they could be on their way if he had told them his suspicions about Ethan.

If the reporter can find him, so can the FBI, which means I am running out of time. Ethan will want to move me soon, and I know I can get out of here.

The next place might be more challenging. I had to prepare for my escape, so I grabbed a stack of images and spread them out with my back to the camera.

I tucked a few pictures under my breasts and went into the bathroom. When I walked out, I faked my hands shaking and went to the tote of snacks.

I opened a sugar packet and dumped it toward my mouth. The crystals slipped past my lips and landed inside my cleavage.

Now that I have all three ingredients, I can make the glue and stick the images together. I sat on the toilet, mixed the goop in my hand, then slapped three pictures together.

Keys rattled near the entrance of my room. He's coming. I snatched the makeshift shim, tucked it under the sink to dry, and sat back on the seat just in time.

"What are you doing in here?"

"Trying to poop. I think I'm constipated," I said, grunting unnecessarily.

"Don't strain. You'll give yourself hemorrhoids. I need to dispose of the trash, and I will get you some stool softeners."

"Thank you," I said to him as I wiped without reason.

Ethan pulled the mattress off the bed, flipped it over and laid it on the floor for me. I curled under the blanket he laid over me and pretended to fall asleep.

Chapter Thirty-One – The Darkroom

A storm took power out again, but when Ethan came downstairs this time, he couldn't reset the camera.

"These storms are supposed to come and go all day and night," he huffed.

"Can I come upstairs with you?"

"Ashley, I have things to do today, and this is the safest place for you," he said, frustrated, as the equipment flicked offline again. "Well, this isn't going to work."

Ethan stared around the room, and his eyes set on the bed. He is thinking about strapping me down, but I almost drowned in my vomit last time.

"Get up," Ethan said, helping me off the mattress.

Ethan walked me over to the chair meant for dining, grabbed a rope from a shelf, and tied me up.

"Ethan, please don't do this. How am I supposed to eat or go pee?"

His hand paused as he thought about the consequences, shifted his glasses onto his nose, and glared at me.

"I've always been able to trust you, so don't make me regret this decision," he said as he untied me. "Can I trust you?"

"Ethan, I promise I won't leave the house," I said, holding three fingers in the air.

He shook his head at my display of sarcasm and walked out. I thought it was funny. If he were to catch me, I wouldn't have broken my word. I never said I wouldn't explore the area beyond my prison.

The moment I heard Ethan's footsteps disappear, I sprang into action. I sprinted into the bathroom, reached under the sink, and pulled out the glued images.

The polaroids came out stiffer than I care for, but they should still flex into the crack between the false door and its frame. I climbed onto the box spring and listened above me for signs of life.

All seemed quiet, so I ran over to the bookshelf and used it like a ladder to get to the moveable tiles. I carefully lifted and slid it to the right and set it back down.

Below me, flakes of ceiling and dirt rained down on the area rug. If he were to come back before I cleaned it, he would know I had left this room. I hopped off the makeshift stairway and cleaned the mess from the floor.

The shelving wobbled as I scaled it and pulled myself into the space between the hall and my room. Three tiles separated me from the other side, and the steel grids bent beneath my weight but held as I lowered into the hallway.

I peered up in the distance to get back up and searched for another way, just in case. A utility shelf sat to the left of my doorway, so I used that to ascend back up and move its tile aside for a quick re-entry.

A red light came from under the room closest to me as I made my way to the secure door at the end of the walkway. The knob turned free as I opened it and peeked inside. A darkroom is lit with several safelight bulbs protecting Ethan's precious photo collection as they are developed.

I walked around a vast table and gawked at image after image of nature, women, and corpses. An array of neatly lined up photos on one side were before, during, and after shots. Picture one is a beautiful woman. She is in distress in picture two. In three and four, the woman is dead, and her body is in decay.

The FBI thought there were only six, but there are ten sets of images here of different women. These do not include the men he has killed so far.

When I rounded the other side of the table, my heart stopped. One of the first images Ethan had taken of me hung in front of my face, smiling happily. I always loved that one, but now it is stained by this moment as I stare at the print beside it.

Ethan's favorite, the one where he was choking me during sex, drifted before my eyes. The gap he left between those two developed pictures and the next ones gave me a startling glimpse into my future.

My fists balled up tightly when I came to the following images. Marilyn, the sweet woman from the bus who helped me, is lying, beaten, and dead. Her broken fingers twisted in unnatural ways, and her fingernails were removed. Ethan took a snapshot of those nails after he shaped them into a colorful smiley face on the pavement.

If I lit it all on fire and ruined his collection, that would piss him off, but I had to be sure I could get out first. The sound of something above made me freeze. Perhaps I am being paranoid, but if he returned and caught me, he would strap me down to the bed for sure.

The feeling that overcame me was unsettling, and I shook. As I worked my way back into the area above, the shelving unit teetered. When I glimpsed at the ground, dust bunnies littered the concrete below.

Blowing down with heaving breaths to disperse them didn't work, so I snatched a how-to manual from the shelf and swooshed it back and forth. It scattered the balls of dirt in all directions and under nearby racks.

After I dropped into my room, I cleaned the floor again, sat at the table, and glanced at the red blinking camera in the corner. I took an apple, rubbed it on my shirt, and took a massive bite as Ethan entered the room.

Juices spilled down my lips as he passed me and set his sights on the surveillance equipment. The status light switched off, flashed blue several times, and returned to green as it came online.

He turned to me and smirked with squinted eyes while tilting his head. The hair on my neck stood at attention as he sat across from me and said nothing. Ethan's suspicious and has every right to be. I continued to eat my apple until he reached over and took it from me.

Ethan toyed with its core after he finished the last few bites and, without warning, struck me in the face with it. I jumped from the table and backed away as blood spilled from my nose.

"Ethan, what was that for?" I said, tipping my head back while pinching the soft part of my nostrils.

He seized my arms and threw me back onto the mattress on the floor. My teeth sank into my tongue when I landed, and now it's bleeding too. Every part of me shook as I became overwhelmed with fear. What if he saw me somehow? What if a footprint is visible, or the tile is crooked, and he noticed?

"Ethan, please stop," I cried. "What did I do?"
"Nothing, yet. I know you and can sense something is off, but I can't quite put my finger on it," he said with his hands on his hips.
"I'm pregnant, Ethan. Everything about me is going to be off," I hissed at him and sobbed.

My hormones took over, and I found my courage. It was not intentional, but I had enough for one day, and after what I saw in his darkroom, I wanted to hurt him. I rolled myself off the ground, stomped toward him, got in his face, and began screaming my feelings.

"Ethan, I'm tired, crampy, and can't stop throwing up. Plus, now my boobs ache all the time. As if I don't have an abundance of other things going on, you're hurting me and causing all this stress. Do you think this is all healthy for Aurora? Do you think hitting her mother and making me bleed won't affect her? Stress affects babies in utero, you asshole. Look it up," I yelled, wiping massive emotional tears from my cheeks.

His face changed from anger to sadness as he thought about what I said. I made him feel guilty, which wasn't my intention, but it worked to my benefit. Ethan came to me, opened his arms, and wrapped them around me in a loving embrace.

"I'm sorry, Ashley."

I pushed him away, rejecting his apology. Ethan didn't deserve my forgiveness. The tears wouldn't stop coming, and I lost the strength to stand. I laid down on the mattress and assumed the fetal position.

Ethan tried to come to me, but I shot him a nasty glance, and he took a step back. My body shook violently, but not from anxiety. I was angry.

"Go, Ethan. Go live your life and do whatever you want. Don't forget to feed me or leave us down here to die."

"I would never do that, Ashley," he said, kneeling beside me.

"Gooooo," I hollered in his face before collapsing onto my bed, continuing to wail.

He staggered back and stood. I thought he might decide to stay with me after my outburst, but he did as I asked and left me alone.

Chapter Thirty-Two – Breaking Point

My depression landed me in hot water with Ethan. I didn't want to eat or drink because I was tired of throwing up and having to pee every two seconds.

Such an inconvenience it all became as I lay in bed on day three with no shower. What is the point? It isn't like I am going anywhere. Who will be around to smell me or see my greasy locks?

"Get up, Ashley, right now," Ethan ordered.
I ignored him and shut my eyes. Ethan seized me under the arms, dragged me into the restroom, and dropped me into a hot bubble bath. I'm not going to lie. It felt fantastic making him pamper me.
If I cared enough, I would thank him, but I feel nothing for him anymore as I stare at his ill-fitting glasses.

"Why are you behaving like this?" He said as he scrubbed my back.

I have no answers for him. My mouth hung open, and I let a few drops of drool escape.
Ethan turned my face to him, and
a slight smile tugged at the corner of my lips, giving away my antics.
A hard slap struck me across the face, and I laughed. I laughed and laughed until I cried as he hit

me a second time, but it didn't stop me. He couldn't kill me because he would lose Aurora, so I continued to cackle.

Bubbles covered my head as he forced my face beneath the surface, but I did not panic. I just smiled with open eyes as he gritted his blurry teeth above the water. He yanked me out by my hair and pulled me out of the tub.

The cold tile felt pleasant on my angry face when I lay down on it. Ethan tried to lift me, but I remained non-compliant, and he became frustrated.

"Dammit, Ashley. Tell me what you want from me?"

"I want to go upstairs and have an actual meal at a proper table like a normal couple," I screamed at him.

"Fine. Get up, and I will make you dinner, but if you try anything stupid, it will never happen again, understand?"

"Yes," I said, smiling a bloody smile at him.

Control is what I have. If I don't eat, it affects Aurora. As far as he knows, I have eaten little in the last several days. Truth be told, I have a stash under the sink with my lock shim.

He unlocked my door, led me up and into the open basement, then up the next set of steps into the kitchen. He tied my ankles and wrists to a chair while he took out all the ingredients to make a lovely meal.

Chicken and mozzarella tortellini alfredo soup and a hearty green salad are on the table in front of me.

He pulled breadsticks from the oven, placed one on my plate, then snatched a candle and lit it.

"Happy now?" Ethan said as he straightened out his napkin before resting it on his lap.

"Are you going to untie me so I can eat it, or should I lean over and chomp it like a pig?" I said, peering at my bound limbs.

He slammed his balled-up fists on the table, threw his napkin off his leg, and stood in front of me. I smiled at him when he kneeled in front of me and used a knife to cut me loose.

Once my hands could move, I rested them on either of his shoulders and whispered, "Thank you, Ethan."

"Eat, Ashley."

I nodded my head and slurped my soup. The buttery smooth flavor welcomed my starving stomach. Ethan sat across from me and watched intently as I clenched the bowl like an animal and drank the rest.

A phone rang in the other room, and I locked eyes with Ethan. He ditched his other phone and got a new one, so who could call him? I tried to listen when he answered, but his voice sounded muffled.

When he returned to the table, he tapped the surface impatiently and glanced at his watch often.

"So, you have a hot date or something?" I asked him as I polished off my breadstick.
"Finish eating."

An alert came across the television for a severe thunderstorm warning in our area. Ethan shut off the device and untied my feet.

"Time to go back," he said, taking me by the arm.
"What about the storm? Aren't you staying with me?"
"Ashley, I have things to do."

As we passed through the lower level, I scanned the room for anything I could use as a weapon.
A small wooden bat leans in the corner by the door, and a metal bar sits inside the track to prevent break-ins. Both were workable options.
Ethan shoved me into my room and secured it. Now that I have a plan, I must wait for the weather to wipe out the internet and hope he is gone when it happens.
He seemed eager for me to finish, and the way he kept glancing at his watch made me think he had a meeting.
His footsteps went from one side of the room to the other, pacing. Is he nervous? If so, about what?

I retrieved my glued polaroids, put them in my bra, shoved a granola bar in my pocket, and laid down, facing the camera. My eyes grew heavy from staring at the light for so long, and I fell asleep.

A thunderous boom startled me back into the world of the living. My eyes darted around the room and stopped at the blinking red status coming from the camera. I threw my house shoes on, used the toilet, and listened to the ceiling for several minutes. Nothing. No noise, no creaks, and no sounds of life.

I scaled the unit, lowered to the other side, walked down the hallway, and climbed into the ceiling to access the stairs leading to the hidden door.

As I reached the top of the steps, I placed my ear against the false door and waited.

My heart pounded so loud that I thought someone would hear it. I took a few deep breaths to calm myself, but my hands wouldn't stop shaking. What if it's a trap? What if he is sitting on the other side of the door waiting for me?

There is no going back now. This storm is my only chance. If I don't take it, I may never have the opportunity again.

I stuffed the bonded images into the crease and pushed. The door popped open, and I peeked through the crack. From what I could see in the dark, the room appeared empty. I opened the door enough to slide through and closed it behind me.

To get out, I must first remove the metal rod securing the door. I took my time and lifted it, striking nothing around it.

Run. That is all I had to do was run. I would have been home free, but the sound of a woman's voice from outside stopped me from taking another step.

Her voice carried from the front of the house to the back, making her seem closer than I thought. Footsteps became louder, along with their voices, as Ethan and an unknown woman entered the house above me.

Glasses rattled in the kitchen, and the distinct pop of a wine cork echoed through the space. He is entertaining another woman, and I feel sorry for her.

My heart raced as fast as my feet as I shot across the lawn like a dog was chasing me. But guilt and unfinished business soon slowed me to a stop. This wasn't the plan.

Ethan is supposed to die, not live on to be with another woman. And what about her? If she dies, her death will be on my hands.

I can't let that happen, won't let it happen. My body bent at the waist, and I rubbed my upper thighs as I contemplated my next move.

Feeling guilty, I let out a breath of fresh night air and stared at the stars. A falling star fell above the house I had just escaped from. Could there be more of a clue what the right thing to do is? I turned on my heels and jogged back toward hell.

Chapter Thirty-Three – Play Ball

My, how the tables have turned. What happened to the sweet innocent Ashley that used to cringe when men yelled and had no voice? I think she died in that dungeon, or perhaps the cave did me in.

I want to be free, that's all. Free to walk the streets, take my daughter to the park, and move on if I choose. Only one obstacle stands in my way, and he drinks wine with another woman in his kitchen. Her hair is dyed the same color as mine, but I don't think Ethan cares about that.

What matters to him is someone who resembles his mother he did not save.

Darkness hides me well below the window I am watching them through. I must wait until the perfect opportunity comes about to strike. Ethan's strength far exceeds my own, so I need to take out his ability to gain the upper hand.

A shed sat next to the house, and I snuck inside to search for something sharp I could use. The sparsely lit space made it difficult to find anything, but I hit the jackpot when I opened a toolbox on the floor.

A quick-change utility knife is just the ticket. I pressed the release button, popped the dull, used side out, and reversed it to a perfectly clean edge.

I grabbed my granola bar, took a giant bite, and headed back to the window. Ethan's getting her drunk, and her short red skirt reminded me of a prostitute as she ran her fingers through his hair.

On the counter next to them sits his 35 mm film camera. He scoops it up and takes pictures of the woman in seductive poses. She hops onto the granite island and spreads her legs for him. Ethan takes a few more shots, then unbuttons his pants, readying himself.

It's time. I crept back in through the back door, grabbed the small wooden bat, took the stairs, and peered around the corner.

Ethan is bare-naked and ramming the woman from behind as she grips the countertop, screaming with pleasure. That is what I wished him to do for me, and here he has just met this woman, and he's giving her what I wanted.

No.

I left the bat by the doorway, crouched onto the tile and crawled my way behind them. Too caught up in his filthy display of lust to see me coming, he never stood a chance.

The blade swiped deeply across both Achilles' tendons, instantly dropping Ethan to his knees. He screamed as he hit the floor and reached down to examine his damaged flesh. The woman flipped around, hollered at the top of her lungs, then ran for the door.

"You forgot your underwear," I yelled, picking them up and throwing them in her direction.

"Ashley, please stop," Ethan pleaded as he stared up at me in disbelief.

I grabbed the bat, and raised it above my shoulders as he covered his head, but my aim was not for that. I came down hard on his oversized balls, using the bat for its intended purpose. Ethan's blood-curdling scream rang through the house like annoying microphone feedback, and vomiting followed.

He stopped talking after that. I grabbed his camera off the granite and snapped a few photos while he cried.

I felt sorry for him for a moment, but it passed as he seized my ankle and tried to pull me off my feet. The bat bounced off the side of his head and shattered as I swung away.

I snatched the camera and took another picture as he panted on the floor.

"Ashley, please. I love you."
"Liar," I shrieked as I straddled his torso and turned his face to mine. "Liar."

His precious equipment became the last thing he would ever see as it came down on his unexpecting eyes. Over and over, I hit him.

All the rage, deception, and abuse flowed from me and onto him in explosive blows as blood splattered across my face. As he bled out, I stopped for a moment, and admired my work.

The gurgling from his throat sounded like a percolating coffee pot as he struggled to breathe.

Sirens blared in the distance as the police made their way to us, but I was not quite finished. I took the camera downstairs and began processing the images. I always wanted my own darkroom thanks to Ethan showing me how satisfying it is to process your own images. He walked me through all the stages and steps until I had it down to a science.

Waiting is the hardest part when you know you have a time constraint. It had only been a few minutes, and many footsteps were trampling the floor above me.

They are coming, but I shut the hidden door to delay them as I moved the images to the next stage of development. The door swung open, and an officer trained his gun on me.

"Police, let me see your hands."

I ignored him and continued developing the pictures. Agent Mills placed her hand on the officer's shoulder so he would stand down. She came and stood beside me, staring at the pictures in the tray.

"I have to finish," I said without looking at her.

Mills nodded in understanding and waited outside the door. A few minutes later, arguing came from out in the hallway as I hung the finished product.

Mr. Johnston barged into the room and came to my side.

I turned to him but didn't have it in me to make eye contact. He rested his fingers under my chin and lifted my face. My world crumbled when I peered into his eyes and collapsed into his arms.

"You're safe now, Ashley," he said as he stroked my hair. "Let's get you upstairs."

"How are you here?" I asked him.

"The FBI couldn't gain access to Ethan's juvenile records. So, I offered to help if I could come."

"I'm glad you did."

Mr. Johnston held me around the waist as we ascended the steps and returned to the kitchen.

The paramedics placed Ethan on a gurney and hoisted him up from the floor. I stood beside him, glaring down at his swollen face, and began to cry. His hand reached for me and clutched me around the throat.

Mr. Johnston grabbed his hand and tried to free it, but Ethan wouldn't let go. We struggled back and forth, then he twisted his body from the gurney and landed on top of me. The vessels in my eyes strained as he crushed my neck in his grip. I bucked underneath him like a bull under a cowboy, but he was too heavy. He is killing us, killing Aurora.

A single gunshot ended all the fighting as Mills put a bullet into Ethan's head. I gasped for air, rolled onto my hands and knees, and began vomiting.

It's over. He's dead, and we are safe now. I gripped my lower abdomen and rocked back and forth as the retching continued. Mr. Johnston stooped before me, pulled a handkerchief from his pocket, and wiped the puke from my distraught lips.

"Thank you."
"You're welcome," he sighed. "How about I take you out of here?"

I nodded as I wept, and he hoisted me off the floor and helped me out of the house.

He sat me down in Mill's vehicle and stood outside with the door open. The coroner took Ethan's body from the house and loaded it into a white van.

I pulled out the glued polaroids from inside my bra and handed them to Mills when she approached with the elephant from Aurora's crib.

"What's this?"
"That is how I escaped the basement."

Mills took them from me as I took the stuffed animal from her. My fingers ran across the letters of my daughter's name. Her name was my choice but the elephant was purchase by Ethan and I wanted no part of it. I threw it over the hood of the car, reached into my pocket and took another bite of the granola bar. Mr. Johnston came over, removed it from my grasp, and tossed it over his shoulder.

"Ashley, why don't we take you to the hospital to get checked out, then clean up, and get some real food in you," Mr. Johnston offered.

"Why?"

"Because a granola bar is not a proper meal. Your baby deserves better," He smiled as he nodded toward my belly.

I smiled back at him. Mr. Johnston was right, it's not, but it helped keep my sugar up and gave me the strength I needed to save us. As we drove to the hospital, I hung my head and played with my blood-stained fingers.

After being evaluated and cleaned up, Mr. Johnston waited outside the room during my ultrasound.

Tears tugged at my eyes as she found the sac and increased the volume. The fetal heart rate came through like music to my ears as the girl explained what I was looking at.

The technician printed an image for me, and I showed it to Mr. Johnston when we were finished.

"She is going to be beautiful, just like her mother," he said as he placed his hand on mine.

"Congratulations, you two. The due date is around July the fourth," the woman said as she was leaving.

I didn't correct her, and neither did Mr. Johnston. Perhaps because our feelings for each other always existed. But I was with Ethan, and Mr. Johnston was always so busy.

Even now, as I stare at our joined hands, there is a level of comfortability that can't be ignored.

"Agent Mills brought some things from your apartment and this," Mr. Johnston said, taking my tattered favorite sweater out of the bag.

"I washed it for you."

"Thank you," I said as a tear dribbled from the corner of my eye, and he wiped it away with his finger.

Our eyes locked, and the room melted away momentarily. Mills entered the room, breaking our focus on each other.

She handed me my discharge papers and told me she would contact me in the next few days to review everything.

Mr. Johnston sat with me while I ate a salad the hospital had sent up to me. My appetite disappeared long before this moment, but I forced myself to eat for Aurora's sake.

Every so often, my hand would shake, and he would steady it with his and remind me that I was safe.

We talked for hours about work, Aurora, and life. By the time I left the hospital, I wanted him to come home with me and keep me company, but I knew I was not ready for that yet.

My thoughts wandered to the red darkroom of graphic images, and I wished I had the time to burn the entire place down. Mr. Johnston saw my sadness and placed his palm on mine.

"What is it?"

"The house. Ethan's parent's house is so full of terrible memories, violence, and death. I hope they tear it down," I said as I stifled a cry.

"Everything is going to be all right," he said, taking my hand and kissing it. "Let's get you home."

Chapter Thirty-Four-Arson

After Mr. Johnston dropped me off, I had difficulty settling in. I'm not comfortable here anymore. Perhaps it is because of all the memories Ethan, and I shared.

In the morning, my first order of business would be to find a place with two bedrooms for Aurora and me.

Mrs. Jones is coming any minute with Ruger, and I'm happy and sad at the same time. He will help the void of my home, but not the one in my heart. I sat on the couch, held a fuzzy white toss pillow, and screamed into it.
Knuckles struck the door several times, and Mr. Johnston stood outside in the hallway, not Ruger and Mrs. Jones, as expected.

"Mr. Johnston, is everything all right?"
"Ashley, can I come in?"
"Of course."

Mr. Johnston entered the room, and his hands rubbed together like they were cold. The long awkward silence told me he wanted to say something but had difficulty spitting it out.

"I need to tell you something that I didn't dare to at the hospital," Mr. Johnston said, taking a breath. "I like you, not just as a friend or employee. Spending time with you is something I enjoy. I will wait for you if you're not ready now because of the circumstances, but I felt it was important to tell you how I feel."

"Mr. Johnston, I don't want you to feel obligated to stay because I have no one else. I enjoy your company, but I am afraid you'll tire of waiting for me to be up for a relationship."

"I don't tire. When I want something, I will fight for it and do whatever it takes. I want you, Ashley, and Aurora. Please give me a chance."

I placed my head against his chest and cried as he held me close. We have worked together for a couple of years, which made it easy to trust him. If it weren't for Ethan, we may have dated and subsequently been together, and none of this would have ever happened.

My level of comfort with him has always been beneath the surface. Mr. Johnston said he wants us both, which means he understands we are a package deal. I hope he accepts Aurora and respects my space during this difficult time.

He took me by the arms and held me away from him, but I refused to make eye contact.

A knock at the door interrupted our moment, and Mr. Johnston went to answer. Ruger flew into the room before he even got the door open. He sprinted around the room, came back, stopped, sniffed my abdomen, and stood before Mr. Johnston. Ruger looked from me to Mr. Johnston as if he was sizing us up or waiting for a cue.

I scratched behind his ears, then Mr. Johnston stooped down on the floor to say hello. Ruger sniffed his hands as if he had caught a whiff of something, then hopped on the couch to lie down.

When he and I joined Ruger on the sofa, he returned to smelling Mr. Johnston's palms.

"I'm sorry, I don't know why he is so fascinated with your hands," I said, taking his hand.

He didn't pull away from me as I inhaled the faint scent of chemicals on his fingers. On the tip of his thumb was a new angry red blister.

"Mr. Johnston, what happened to your finger?"
"Burned it."

As soon as he answered, a news report came across the television.

'The former family home of the notorious Cavern Killer went up in flames. Sources inside the fire department believe arson may have caused the blaze. Details are still coming in on this breaking story, and we will keep you updated....'

My heart leaped into my throat, and my eyes widened as I realized what he had done.

"Mr. Johnston?"

"I told you whatever it takes," he said, drawing me close and rubbing my shoulder.

"What if they find out?"

"They won't."

Another knock made us both stop talking. I removed his arm from me and took my time getting to the door. When I peered through the peephole, Mills was standing in the hall.

"Ashley, did you hear the news?"

"I did. How crazy is that?"

"Sorry, but I have to ask, where have you been since you left the hospital?"

"Here. I had to wait for Ruger to be brought back by Mrs. Jones."

"Can anyone corroborate your story?" Mills asked as she scanned the apartment.

"I can," Mr. Johnston said, exiting the bathroom.

"You're still here," she said, raising her eyebrows.

"Yes. We were about to rent a movie. Would you like to stay and join us?" Mr. Johnston offered as he removed a bag of popcorn from the microwave.

"No, thank you. So, you two came here after the hospital and never left?"

"That's right," Mr. Johnston lied, so I didn't have to.

"Excellent. Well, I will leave you two to your movie. Ashley, I will stop by and get your statement for the file tomorrow."

"Sounds like a plan."

Mills walked over to the door and glimpsed at us one last time. She felt our deception, but what does it matter now? The killer is dead. All the evidence was removed from the house before the blaze, so the case was closed as far as we were concerned.

Mr. Johnston and I stared at the television screen as another report came in about the fire. This time they have a video. He handed me the popcorn, and we smiled while watching Ethan's former home burn to the ground.

Although getting my wish was breathtaking, it would be terrible if they learned about Mr. Johnston's involvement. He got up, walked to his jacket, and pulled something from the interior pocket.

"I bought something for you on my way here,"

It was a manual about what to expect while you're pregnant. Inside, it showed the stages of pregnancy, the symptoms that went along with each trimester, and the comparison of your baby to external objects.

A tear tugged at the corner of my eye as I focused on the size comparison of Aurora now. She's a tadpole. Tiny and cute, with a little tailbone. Mr. Johnston took the book from me and opened it.

"What are you doing?" I smiled, trying to take it back from him.

"I thought we could go over it together. That way, I know as well," he said as he read page one.

'Together…'

Mr. Johnston is already trying to prepare for what is coming and how to cope. I don't know how deserving I am of such kindness and understanding. I was broken and thought no one could ever want to be with me after what had happened. Perhaps it is all in my head.

Aurora's ultrasound image rested on the coffee table, and Mr. Johnston picked it up. He grinned as he held it and then gazed deep into my eyes.

"I can't wait to meet her," he said, nodding.
"Me too."

Mr. Johnston smacked his thighs, and I laid my head on his lap. As the movie began, I closed my eyes. There couldn't be a more perfect ending to my day. Despite Ethan's death, I didn't experience an enormous sense of loss, for I had gained so much more.

Though we still have a long road, I am confident Mr. Johnston will be here to take this rough ride with me. I fell asleep on his leg as he stroked my hair and dreamed of our future together. Mr. Johnston will make a fantastic father even though he's not Auroras' biological one.

Blood does not always make you a good parent, which I'm sure Ethan knew far too well before he took his last breath.

The End

Epilogue

Mr. Johnston and I are on a first-name basis now. Calling him Mike is so much easier. I never returned to the office because of the publicity of everything. Working from home made more sense.

Mike comes by my new two-bedroom home every day after work, picks up the day before workload, and drops off my newest assignments.

Sometimes, he stays, and we have dinner and watch a movie, but mostly he tries to give me my space. Our slow-moving relationship has grown like my abdomen, stretching a little further each day.

We have made love a handful of times in the last seven months, and it felt amazing. It was everything I had hoped for. I'd give him so much more, but my discomfort far outweighed my desire these days.

At my last ultrasound, they said Aurora was tucked in and ready to go soon. Little did I know that soon meant today as I stood before Mike with a puddle beneath me.

"Shit," I said, looking at him with a shocked look.

"Oh my God," Mike said as he darted from room to room, gathering my hospital and diaper bags.

"Mike, call for help," I said as I lowered my body to the floor.

"What? Why? The hospital isn't that far."

"Aurora is not waiting," I said as a painful contraction struck me like a kick to the abdomen and back.

The overwhelming urge to push came shortly after, and it took everything in my power not to as Mike spoke frantically to the emergency dispatcher.

Mike grabbed a pile of towels and sat next to me.

"Ashley, I have to take off your bottoms," he said, waiting for permission.

"Okay," I said through clenched teeth.

He placed a clean towel under my naked rear end and neatly stacked the extras beside my now-bent knees. His eyes widened as the dispatcher gave him the next set of instructions.

"She said with your next contraction, push, and I will guide her out," he said as sweat rolled down his face.

"It's too early, Mike. What if something is wrong?"

"The dispatcher said to let you know the ambulance is only a few miles away and will be here any minute. You are only five weeks early, and babies come that early all the time and are just fine," he said nervously.

Another pain came to me, and it felt like my stomach, back, and vagina split into multiple pieces. I screamed through it as Mike yelled for me to push hard.

Tears filled his eyes as the faint cry of a baby came from between my legs. He quickly grabbed towels and yelled to the dispatcher over speakerphone that Aurora had arrived. He wrapped her up carefully and then helped me get on my side. Once there, he placed her next to me so I could see her.

"She's so beautiful," I cried. "Hello, Aurora. I am your mommy."

A sudden stabbing pain startled me and made her cry.

"It's the placenta. They said it needs to deliver, too," Mike said, reassuring me.

He gagged as the afterbirth tumbled onto the carpet, looking like pizza with no cheese. Mike took a towel and pushed it next to Aurora.

"I'm sorry, Ashley. I know it is gross, but they said it must stay at the same level."

"I don't care. She is all that matters now," I said, kissing her vernix-covered hand.

More titles by this author

The Unnerving
Sidero
The Carpenter's Chameleon–Book Two of Sidero

In loving memory of my mother,

Blanche "Bonnie" Folwell.

A very special thank you to Robert Harrison, RW Harrison Books, for your kindness and willingness to help a new author.

If you read and enjoyed my book, I'd really appreciate a review!
Thank you.

It was hard to tell while wet, but her hair appeared strawberry blonde and not fire red like mine, but I didn't care. She is perfect in every way.

Mike turned on his side and lay down next to us. He took Aurora's other hand and talked to her as though she were his own. How she looked at him, as though she knew him already, made me confident that I made the right choice in letting him into our lives.

He reached over, swiped a tear from my cheek, and whispered.

"You're going to be an amazing mom."

The paramedics tapped on the unlocked door, and Mike told them to enter. They took us to the hospital via ambulance and brought Aurora in after a pediatrician evaluated her.

"She's a fighter, that's for sure," the pediatrician said, handing her to Mike.
"Just like her mother," Mike said as his eyes welled, and he hummed to her softly.